# Short H
# Stories

# Collections IV - VI

# P.J. Blakey-Novis

*Enjoy the nightmares!.*

*PBN*

0

DISCLAIMER: "This is a work of fiction. Names, characters, places and incidents are products of the author's imagination and are used fictitiously. Any resemblance to actual events, locales or persons, living or dead, is entirely coincidental."

Copyright © 2021 Red Cape Publishing

All rights reserved.

*Collection IV: Karma* ©2019

*Collection V: The Place Between Worlds* ©2020

*Collection VI: Home* © 2021

Cover Design by Red Cape Graphic Design

www.redcapepublishing.com/red-cape-graphic-design

*Fossil Bluff* first published in *Black Dogs, Black Tales, Things in the Well,* 2020

*The Place Between Worlds* first published in *Stuff of Nightmares,* 2019

*Passing Through* is featured on the Indipenned website and was the winner of the Indipenned Short Story Contest 2020

*Quake* first published in *Elements of Horror: Earth,* 2019

*Deep Breaths* first published in *Elements of Horror: Air,* 2019

*The Flames of Hell Are Coming* first published in *Elements of Horror: Fire,* 2019

*Home* first published in *Elements of Horror: Water,* 2019

For Leanne
Always my biggest supporter.

# Contents

Coven

Karma

Night Terrors

Riddles and Rewards

Teenage Kicks

Trailer Trashed

Fossil Bluff

The Devil's Triangle

The Place Between Worlds

Six Reasons to Live

I Lived for Too Long

Passing Through

Quake

Cemetery of the Living

Deep Breaths

Shielded

The Flames of Hell Are Coming

Burt's Rage

Home

Dark Waters

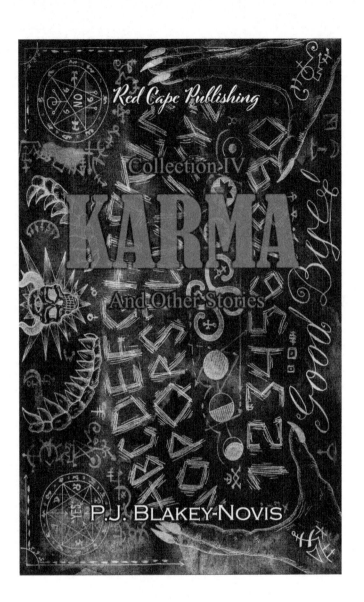

Red Cape Publishing

Collection IV

KARMA

And Other Stories

P.J. BLAKEY-NOVIS

# Coven

"I'll need you to tell me everything," the court appointed lawyer told me, without even a *hello*. "You need to be completely honest with me, or I can't offer you proper counsel." I knew I was screwed, and being represented by this overweight, sweaty mess wasn't going to change anything.

"What's the point?" I asked, yanking my hands up from the table to bring his attention to the stainless-steel cuffs which were digging into my wrists.

"The point, Miss Price, is that a good defence could mean the difference between a prison sentence or the death penalty. And the fact that I was court appointed does not mean I don't know what I'm doing. So, if you want to live, I suggest you start at the beginning." I huffed, but I knew he had a point. At the age of nineteen, I still hadn't grown out of throwing strops.

"Sarah," I said. "Call me Sarah. And what do you need to know? Other than the fact they are all dead because of me."

"I need to know everything. What happened to the others? How did you end up there? Why did you do it? I know you intend to plead guilty, as is your right, but if there is anything we can use as mitigating circumstances then it could go a long way to reducing your sentence. Or could lead to you being held at a different facility." I looked at him with a scowl.

"An asylum, you mean?" He shifted his gaze uncomfortably.

"We don't use that term, Miss... Sarah," he stated. "I meant somewhere that may be able to help you, if that's what is required."

"What's your name?" I asked him, fixing him with a stare. He held up his lanyard.

"Gerry? That short for Gerald?" I asked. He continued to look uncomfortable, sweat soaking through his shirt. He simply nodded. "I had a book about a giraffe called Gerald when I was little," I told him.

"Can we start to discuss your case please Sarah?"

"I thought you wanted to know everything?" I replied, smugly. "That book is my earliest memory, I think. You want everything, then that is where it starts." Gerry opened his notebook and clicked on his pen.

"How long have you lived at the address on Montgomery Street?" he asked, glancing up at me from his notebook.

"Always," I replied. "At least, for as long as I can remember."

"Which school did you attend?"

"I was home-schooled," I told him. "I'm sure all that must be on record somewhere." He made notes on the paper.

"And the other people who lived there, who were they to you?"

"Family, of course," I explained, unsure why he had even asked that question.

"You were related to all of the residents of that house? By blood?" he asked, already knowing the answer.

"Have you even looked at my file?" I asked, becoming frustrated already. "You should know all this shit. My dad was a scumbag who bailed when my mum got pregnant. My mum died of an overdose when I was two, and I went to live with Shona."

"And Shona is a relation of your mother's?" he asked.

"They were pretty much sisters, from what I've been told. Best friends, you know? So, Shona raised me, with the others."

"Others?" Gerry asked, still scribbling. "The other women, or where there more children?"

"A couple of them were children when they moved in, but older than me. Deborah is, was, twenty-six. I think Sandy was about the same age."

"You're nineteen now?" Gerry asked. I nodded.

"So, when you arrived at the house at the age of two, Deborah and Sandy would have been around nine." I mumbled confirmation, although this was not really a question; Gerry was just thinking aloud. "Tell me about the adults at the house, the people who were already adults when you began living there seventeen years ago." At this point he stopped scribbling and looked at me. I sighed, just wanting this over with.

"Okay, so there was Shona, Margaret, Marie, and Kim. Kim wasn't her real name, she's Chinese or something and it was the closest to it, so everyone went with that. Shona was in charge, like I said."

"And what did being in charge involve?" Gerry asked, interrupting me. I paused, unsure how to answer what seemed like a ridiculous question.

"Well, she dealt with all the household stuff, I guess. Bills, and so on. She gave everyone their chores to do. Everyone looked up to her, respected her, I suppose. And she taught me some of my lessons."

"You may not know," Gerry said, "but were you taught from the standard curriculum?" I shrugged.

"Margaret taught me music; piano, cello, and violin. Marie covered English and Math. Kim taught me self-defence..." At this point Gerry looked back up from the pad he had been scribbling in.

"Self-defence?" he questioned. How was I to know that wasn't taught at normal schools.

"Yeah, they all insisted I'd need it when I was older so that was a regular thing for the last ten years or so."

"And what did Shona teach?"

"I suppose it doesn't matter now," I sighed. "Shona taught the dark arts."

"As in? Magic?" Gerry asked, successfully hiding any surprise if he felt any.

"Do you believe in magic, Gerry?" I asked.

"Do you?" he countered. I knew this conversation would have landed me in all kinds of trouble with Shona, but she wasn't around to do anything about it and my situation was pretty dire.

"What do you think?" I asked. "Of course I do! You can't be raised by a coven of witches and have any doubts." There, it was out. Now there was a good chance I'd end up in an institute, but it was the truth. I watched Gerry write the word *witches* and underline it twice.

"What led to the events of last Friday?" he asked. Although I knew this was coming, I couldn't help a tear escaping down my cheek.

"I wanted to leave. Not move out, I knew that would never happen, but I had a date," I told him, sheepishly. I knew how it sounded; a petulant teenager sulking for not being allowed to go out with a boy. But I was nineteen and I had needs.

"You're an adult, Sarah. Could you not just leave?"

"You think I could have gone against a group of five witches and just waltzed out the door?" I asked, incredulously. "It doesn't work like that."

"So, how does it work? If they were that powerful, and you're so helpless, how come you are here, and they are all in the morgue?" Gerry asked.

"I'm far from helpless!" I told him, my voice rising. "I meant that I couldn't just leave the house, without forcing them to let me."

"I've seen the crime scene photos, Sarah. The house was a bloodbath. I know you have confessed, but in all honesty, I find it hard to believe you did that all by yourself." *Don't mention Robby,* I told myself. "The police don't think you've acted alone, either. If you think you are protecting someone then you really need to consider what you are telling me. If the police find evidence of an accomplice, then it means you have lied in your confession and that could have serious repercussions."

"Whatever I tell you is confidential, right? You can only advise me, not grass me up to the cops?" Gerry didn't look pleased with the phrasing of my question, but he nodded anyway. "Fine, Robby was there. But he didn't do anything. We had planned to go out and he came to the house to pick me up."

"Just so I'm clear, how did you meet this Robby person? It sounds as though the ladies you lived with had you on quite a tight leash."

"How does anyone meet anyone these days?" I asked. "The Internet. When he came to the house it was the first time we had met in person; up to that point we'd only chatted online."

"So, you met someone online, became friendly, and arranged to go on a date. When did you tell Shona and the others about this?"

"On Friday. I was dreading it but hoped they would understand."

"But they didn't?"

I shook my head sadly. "Shona sent me

to my room and placed a spell on the windows and doors so that I could not leave." I knew what I was saying was the truth, but Gerry didn't look convinced in the slightest. "Then Robby turned up, and all hell broke loose." I began to sob, trying to get events in a clear order. "I heard the doorbell ring, but no one made a move to answer it. It rang a few more times with the same result. My bedroom window looked out from the front of the house and I stood at it, banging on the glass, crying. Robby saw me, and knew something was wrong so he kept on banging on the front door until Shona gave in. I heard the door open and talking coming from downstairs. I thought this was my chance; the others were desperate to hide their true nature from 'normal' people, so I didn't think they would try to stop me leaving with Robby present." I couldn't control the tears by this point, and Gerry briefly left the room to fetch some tissues. Once he had settled back into his chair and I had cleaned up my face as best I could, I continued.

"Shona told Robby that I wasn't allowed to go out, but he insisted that he check on me. I ran down the stairs and grabbed his hand, pulling him towards the door, hopeful that I could deal with any trouble I'd be in when I got home. Shona lost her temper, reinstating the spell, and making the door impossible to open. The idea that it was witchcraft didn't enter Robby's head, until Shona began chanting, quickly joined by the others. I recognised the spell as one I had been taught early on; it's used to make people forget what they have seen. Shona always said it was an important one, in case our cover was ever compromised. Robby just stared as the spell began to take hold, and I knew Shona would completely erase his memory of me, as well as that evening. Deborah and Sandy approached me from either side, grabbing an arm each and shoved me towards the stairs. I saw red. Purple lines began to show along my arms as something welled inside me, a defensive instinct taking over. Fight or flight, I suppose, but with flight not an option I had little choice. Both girls had had the same self-defence training that I had, but they weren't expecting me to attack. I felt invincible as an energy flowed through my body and I brought my arms together throwing Deborah and Sandy into one another. Before anyone could stop me, I reached forward, snapping both of their necks in turn, and dropping their corpses to the floor." Gerry looked up from his notes, smiled nervously, and asked me to continue.

"Shona was still in some kind of trance with Robby, and they both seemed unaware of what was happening. Margaret, Marie, and Kim looked shocked and hesitated for a moment. I knew as soon as Shona was back in the room, mentally, I mean, that the consequences would be serious. There was no going back, and I worked through them liked a crazed animal."

"You killed them all?" Gerry asked. "What was Robby's role in this?"

"I used a spell which works a bit like a teleportation device, but its range is limited to only a few metres. I disappeared and reappeared in the kitchen, grabbing two knives from the block on the counter. Then repeated the process to appear directly behind the three women. I knew Kim would be the most difficult opponent, so I thrust both knives into her neck, one on each side. I slashed in a frenzy, taking Marie and Margaret down without any difficulty. That just left Shona."

"She was decapitated," Gerry stated. "By you?"

"That's right," I said. I wasn't proud of my behaviour, but there was little point in trying to deny it now. "She came out of her trance, just about having time to see the carnage around her before I lunged at her throat. As I said earlier, she was a powerful witch, but I had the element of surprise. The first knife struck its target, puncturing her windpipe. She managed to reel off a quick spell which launched me into the air, but she could not get the words out for another. I watched as she struggled to breathe, and I'll admit that I enjoyed the feeling of power. As she took her last breath, I knelt beside her, kissed her forehead, and removed her head before placing it on the table. It was only then that my gaze shifted to Robby. His face was pale, and he'd pissed himself, but he stayed rooted to the spot."

"But you let him leave?" Gerry asked.

"Of course! And that was the painful part of that evening. I cast a spell to make him forget what he had seen, to make him forget he had been there, even to forget about me. Everyone was dead, and I didn't even get to go on my date. It doesn't look like I'll be going on one any time soon, either. So, what happens now?" I asked Gerry.

"Don't take this the wrong way, Sarah, but my advice would be to enter a plea of insanity."

"You think I'm making this up, or that it's nonsense but I still believe it, and therefore I'm mad?"

"I probably shouldn't say this, but the truth is fairly irrelevant. What you have told me is *your* truth, but a judge may well deem that as a sign of mental illness. And an institute would be more comfortable than prison. We can certainly play on your unorthodox upbringing and claim that you have been damaged by Shona and the other women who raised you. Just think about it, and I'll be by in a few hours." Gerry's chair gave a creak of relief as he stood from it and approached the door. He paused, and I guessed what he was going to say before the words left his mouth. "If this teleportation spell of yours works, then why are you still sat there?" Instantaneously I was in front of him, close enough to smell his breath. His eyes widened in fear, but he did not speak.

"I'm still here, Gerry, because I felt as though I deserved to be punished. But perhaps you are right, I am just a product of my environment. Shona made me this way, and now she's dead. My mum was a junkie. The only relative I assume is still alive is my dad."

"But you can't leave?" Gerry stammered.

"Of course I can," I told him with a smile, and I was gone.

# Karma

Two days, trying to hide. Sleeping in a cave, pissing against trees, shivering as I refused to light a fire. It took me less than a day to realize they wanted me dead. Bloody women. I didn't end up here by accident; they knew what they were doing. The punishment fits the crime, I guess. Seven women died at my hands; it was only right that I died at theirs. There was no human way for them to know what I did, I was too careful. But those that took me away, those that brought me to this place, were far from human. From a distance, they appeared as human women, but perhaps sirens would be more apt. Seductive, beautiful, deadly.

They could have killed me on that first night, as I collapsed, naked and vulnerable. My ego had gotten the better of me, no alarm bells ringing when two women showed an interest in sharing my bed that night. We got as far as a few kisses and the removal of clothes, mine anyway, before it all goes hazy. From my small apartment on London's South Bank to here, wherever here may be. I've always hated nature; the smell, the lack of any form of convenience. However, here I awoke, slumped against a rock, head groggy, teeth chattering in an attempt to warm me and counteract the icy downpour which beat against my exposed flesh.

I must have sat there for an hour, at least, trying to understand my predicament. Someone, or some thing, wanted to hurt me. I'd killed, a number of times, and somehow they knew; it was the only motive I could come up with, albeit a rather major one. When I finally made it to my feet, searching for shelter, I saw one of them move. For the briefest of moments, a form darted across the tree-line in front of me. Unmistakably female, but with an otherworldly presence that seemed to launch her through the greenery. I ran, my bare feet feeling every stab from the undergrowth, until I thought I was out of sight. Out of breath, with blood-soaked feet, I slumped down on a fallen tree trunk. I allowed my eyes to close for the briefest of moments, before I heard the whiz of arrows. Three, in quick succession, stabbed their way into the wood not an inch to my left. Relief washed over me, stupidly thinking my attackers had missed, knowing now that they were merely toying with me.

I willed myself on, blocking out the pain

in my legs and feet, finally sliding down a muddy bank where I hoped I was out of sight. Leaves rustled all around, and I could not decide if it was the wind, or these creatures, but nothing came. I slept in that mud, woken several hours later by the sun peering through the canopy. My eyes adjusted to the light, picking out the silhouettes of women stood high in the trees, watching me silently. They wanted me to run, and I did. Perhaps a better man would have stood up to them, demanded an explanation, but that was not me. I killed women, but the roles had been reversed, and I was finally afraid.

There was no choice other than to go further into the forest, but I knew that I was only delaying the inevitable. Each turn I took was watched by my demons, ever silent. The occasional arrow would shoot past me, always close enough to remind me they were there. The day turned to dusk, and I was overwhelmed by thirst. My body knew what it needed, and water became my priority. The rain had barely stopped, and all I could do was consume the little puddles found on leaves; it was that, or muddy water. I gave up running, knowing that my body could no longer keep up the pace, and I had not put any distance between myself and my hunters. I walked through the darkness, waiting for the arrow to finally find its target.

I came across a cave. It took some consideration, as I knew I could be seen, and therefore knew I would be cornering myself. I wanted shelter and, deciding that they could have killed me at any point so far, I took the chance. I don't remember falling asleep, but it is no surprise that it would have been quick. Once again, I awoke to the sun piercing through the entrance. It would have been far brighter had they not been stood at the entrance; seven deadly sirens, finally making their move. I sat up, now shaking with fear, trying to see their faces. They stepped closer. There was an edge of familiarity. They were not beautiful, nor were they living. The dark-haired, dark-skinned creature closest to me grinned. Three or four teeth were missing, the left side of her face swollen from the hammer blows I had inflicted. Two more stepped nearer, crimson lines across their throats from my hunting knife. Now I understood.

In a blur, they descended upon me, clawing at my naked body. I closed my eyes instinctively, hearing the popping sounds as my arms were torn from their sockets. It felt as though flesh were being ripped from my legs. Something, a hand presumably, dug its way inside me through my belly. My death was brutal, but so had theirs been, and karma came for me in the end.

# Night Terrors

Sleeping had never been a problem for me. To be honest, I felt tired most of the time, but I put that down to a combination of my age and having a very busy lifestyle. So, as soon as my head hit the pillow each evening, I'd be out like a light, not waking again until my 6.30am alarm began to scream at me. My wife, despite also insisting that she was 'just as tired', managed to squeeze in an hour or two of reading each night, something I would like to have done but never really tried.

Therefore, it was strange to wake during the night. I reluctantly lifted one eyelid and waited for the brilliant red numerals to come into focus - 2.44am. I stirred, listening out for whatever could have disturbed my sleep, my eyes again firmly closed. *Perhaps someone had slammed a car door outside, or a motorbike had passed by?* Whatever it had been, there was no sound now and my wife had slept through it. I must have been quickly off again, but that slight disturbance seemed to add to my exhaustion the next morning.

I dragged myself from beneath the duvet, the chill of winter having seeped its way into the house, fighting for power over the central heating. Grabbing my dressing gown, I slowly moved towards the kitchen, eyelids heavy, and clicked on the kettle. *The first day of the working week, and I'm this tired already,* I thought, knowing that my mood would not be a good one for the rest of the day. My usual routine was so well practiced that I was almost on autopilot. I made a coffee for myself, a tea for my wife, and powered up my laptop. She drank her tea in bed, whilst I sat at the desk to check my emails in preparation for arriving at the office. I showered, dressed, kissed my wife goodbye, and left the house.

Monday ran through in its usual mundane way, and it had felt like an eternity before the clock on my office wall finally hit 5pm. Without hesitation, I grabbed my coat and hurried out of the building, not bothering to say farewell to any of my colleagues. After all, I'd be seeing them all again in the morning. I was home by 6pm, as with every week day, and was greeted by the smell of dinner cooking. Eyeing my wife pottering around our small kitchen, I felt something akin to pride. I knew I was a lucky man. After we had exchanged our pleasantries, summarised how each of our days had gone, and consumed the delicious meal that she had prepared, I told her about last night. It was bugging me, and had been all day, but I was unsure as to why.

"Something woke me up last night," I told her. "About a quarter to three. It's made me more tired than usual."

"Even more tired than usual?" she asked, her tone teasing. "Well, you should get straight to bed now then."

"I'd like to, actually, but it's only just after eight," I replied. It was then that I caught the look in her eyes, a mischievous twinkle as she took my hand.

"Then maybe *we* should go up to bed," she said, leading me upstairs before I could answer. We made love enthusiastically for almost an hour, something I had been too tired to do for several weeks, and we drifted off to sleep in each other's arms, both satisfied and content.

*Monday*

As I was falling asleep, I felt a relief that it was at least an hour earlier than usual and hoped this would make up for the previous night's disturbance. When I did awaken, I was sitting upright. I must have had a dream, but I could not recall it, however my heart was racing, and my hands shook. The room was in complete darkness, the only light emanating from the alarm clock's blinding red numbers. I glanced towards it, hoping that it was almost time to get up. I frowned when the numbers became clear; 2.44am. *What are the chances of that?* I pondered. Slowly, I lay back down, and placed an arm around my wife, causing her to stir. My heart was still beating faster than usual, and I felt a little odd. I could not explain why, but something felt *wrong*.

"You okay?" she mumbled, eyes still closed.

"Yeah," I told her. "I think I had a nightmare, can't really remember." She was too sleepy to reply again, and I did my best to get back to sleep despite the eerie feeling. Upon returning to sleep, which must have happened quickly, whatever nightmare had awoken me continued. When I was finally disturbed by the alarm clock, I was drenched in sweat, shaken, and all too aware of the details of my dream. Death had come for me in my dreams, in the guise of a tall figure, perhaps the Grim Reaper himself. In this horrific nightmare, I had heard the floorboards in my bedroom creak as heavy boots entered the room and, peering from beneath my duvet, I had been able to make out the silhouette of someone, or something. Transfixed on what I saw before me, unable to move, I watched as the intruder stood in silence above me for several minutes, before a blackened hand lunged from beneath his cloak towards my face. Thankfully, my alarm clock pulled me back to reality just in time.

The dream haunted me for the entire day, affecting my ability to concentrate at work, and putting me on edge. My colleagues noticed that something was wrong, commenting that I seemed to be distracted, which I shrugged off as just being tired. It wasn't a lie, for I did feel exceptionally tired, but I could hardly tell them I'd had a bad dream, or I'd be ridiculed. I did, however, attempt to explain the dream to my wife over dinner.

"It was horrible," I complained. "I know it was only a dream, but I was shaking, and sweating. You know those dreams that are so vivid that it seems real, even once you have woken up?" She nodded, looking at me with a mild level of concern. "I haven't been able to stop thinking about it all day, and now it's making me worry about going to sleep tonight."

"The more you think about it, the more likely you are to dream about it. You know that. So, let's have some wine and find a comedy to watch for a bit, until you are almost falling asleep. You'll be fine," she promised. I wasn't so sure, but what she said made sense and I went along with it. We chose to watch a romantic comedy which was more amusing than I had expected, and cleared two bottles of red wine between us, so I was more than ready to sleep by ten o'clock. My wife placed her arms around me as we found comfortable positions and, once again, I was soon in a deep sleep.

*Tuesday*

Sleep came easily, but so did the nightmares, different, yet similar. I awoke with a scream, glancing at the clock, and was less surprised this time to see that it read 2.44am. Less surprised, but even more terrified. Reaching over to my left for the comfort of my wife, I found her side of the bed empty, panic rising within me. Pulling back the bed covers, a chill came over me. More than a chill, in fact; it was as though a window had been left open in the middle of winter. I could see my breath and I stood, reaching for my dressing gown. I resisted the urge to call out her name but made my way to the spare room assuming she would be there. The room was untouched, as it had been for months. In the thick darkness, I felt my way carefully down the stairs, my eyes gradually adjusting to the lack of light. As I reached the bottom of the stairs, I saw a fragment of light shining through the gap beneath the door to the living room.

Still feeling on edge, and afraid of something indescribable, I pushed the door open slowly. The lamp in the corner of the room was on, and there was a welcoming warmth inside. My wife, wrapped in a cotton throw, was asleep on the sofa with an open book lying on her chest. I sat beside her, placing a hand on her exposed thigh, startling her. She pulled away quickly, looking around the room in confusion.

"Your hands are freezing!" she said.

"Sorry," I mumbled. "The bedroom is really cold too. I woke up at 2.44 again, and you weren't there. I was worried."

"I wasn't there," she explained, "because you were moving about too much in your sleep, making noises. It sounded like you were having a bad dream again, but I didn't see any point in waking you up."

"I was dreaming something, but it's all a bit muddled. Some kind of man, or a creature maybe, came into the bedroom."

She looked at me with some sympathy, before suggesting we go back up to bed. She turned off the living room lamp, and switched on the hallway light, before leading me back upstairs. The room still felt cold, but my wife did not seem to notice, and she buried herself beneath the duvet. I wanted to leave a light on, but despite the fear that I felt, I knew how ridiculous it sounded. So, I opted for trying to stay awake instead. I watched the numbers on the alarm clock change, painfully slowly, until the hour had moved from two, to five. As early as that was, it was not unreasonable to get up, and the sooner I could turn on the lights the better.

I spent the early hours pottering about the house, slowly preparing myself for the working day ahead. I sat with a coffee, toying with the idea of calling in sick, but decided against it. There was nothing to be gained by staying at home, apart from the opportunity to sleep, but that was the one thing I wanted to avoid. I felt anxious, unable to shake the feeling that something terrible was about to happen, even though I told myself how illogical that was. I kept myself as busy as possible, passed the hours away in the office as best I could, and made my way home once again. *If tonight is no better then a trip to the doctor may be needed,* I told myself, wondering whether sleeping pills would stop the nightmares. *But first, I need to get through tonight.* A sense of dread came over me as the evening moved on quickly, the hours disappearing, and the unavoidable darkness approaching.

*Wednesday*

As I prepared myself for bed, brushing my teeth, undressing, and so forth, I noticed a tremble beginning in my hands. My palms felt clammy, my pulse quickening, and a wave of nausea swept over me. *This is ridiculous,* I told myself. *It's just a bloody dream.* My wife could see how anxious I felt, but there was a look of helplessness in her eyes. She knew there was little she could do to comfort me, just as much as I knew that I had to endure these terrors in solitude.

Despite the overwhelming amount of tiredness I felt, sleep did not come easily. Fear had sunken its claws deep within me, and my body did everything it could to fight against what I knew would come. The last time I recall looking at the clock was at almost midnight, and my wife had already fallen asleep. It must have been

31

soon after this time that I finally nodded off. It wasn't a dream that woke me this time, nor did I open my eyes in blind panic or cold sweats. I woke to my wife gently shaking me, whispering in the darkness. It took me a few moments to register what she was telling me.

"There is someone at the door," she said quietly. I looked to the clock, the familiar numbers glaring at me in their bloody redness - 2.44am.

"There can't be," I told her, not as confidently as I had hoped.

"I heard someone," she continued. She sounded frightened, and so I attempted to hide my own fears. Had the light been on, she would surely have noticed the ghostly shade of white I had turned. I had no doubt that something was outside, and I knew that there was no way my wife would go back to sleep without me investigating.

My legs felt heavy as I swung them over the side of the bed, as if they were afraid to leave the perceived safety of the duvet. A little unsteadily from both tiredness and nervousness, I made my way on to the landing and flicked on the light. My eyes closed slightly in response, gradually becoming used to the glare. I was certain that if someone, or something, was waiting at the door, then it would not be friendly.

As I took the final step, I glanced around for something to use as a weapon but could only find an umbrella. It would be unlikely to be much use, but I felt a tiny bit more powerful with it in my hand.

I could see nothing through the frosted glass of the front door; no shadow of someone waiting, no light of any kind. *If* there had been someone there, they must surely have gone. Knowing that I had to open the door in order to satisfy my wife, I moved my free hand towards the keys to unlock it. My heart raced, my hand moving more slowly than I wanted, before making contact. The cold metal of the keys touched my skin at the same moment that something struck the glass of the door. I jumped, falling backwards, and kicking myself away from the door.

The security light, which comes on whenever someone approaches the door, gave no illumination. I stared at the glass, breathing heavily, waiting in the silence for something to happen. Nothing came; no bang on the door, no movement outside, just stillness. I heard footsteps behind me, causing me to startle again, and was relieved to find my wife standing at the bottom of the stairs.

"What happened?" she asked, confusion on her face as she looked down at me sprawled across the floor, umbrella still in hand.

"I went to open the door, but something banged on the glass. Scared the crap out of me."

"Have you been out there?" she asked, looking at the door nervously.

"I was about to, but I don't think there is anyone there. I couldn't see anyone through the glass, and the light hasn't come on."

"Just have a quick look please," she asked, much to my despair. "It was probably some drunks on the way home, but I won't be able to sleep if we haven't at least checked it out." *You won't be able to sleep!* I thought but kept the words to myself. My face must have given me away, however, as she stepped over me, towards the door. "Geez, I'll do it." I still did not move, and I felt a pang of embarrassment for being so cowardly. I watched intently as she reached for the set of keys, expecting something to crash against the glass again but there was only silence. I heard the lock click and watched as my wife pulled open the front door. She was greeted by only darkness and a bone-numbing chill in the air.

"Nothing there," she said, turning to me as I began to stand, the door remaining

34

open behind her. "Let's get back to bed." I began to climb the stairs as I heard the door close and the keys turn in the lock. Something caught my eye on the way to the bedroom, a reflection in one of the picture frames, something dark behind her. I turned quickly, seeing only my wife following me up the stairs. *It's just the lack of sleep,* I told myself, but I knew this was a lie.

*Thursday morning*

My alarm screeched at me, forcing me from my slumber. It was still dark, and exhaustion had left my eyelids heavy. It took a matter of seconds to decide that I would be calling in sick to work. I turned to the spot where my wife should have been sleeping, only to find it empty. *I must have been disturbing her again,* I guessed, hoping to find her in the spare room. The sofa bed which we use on the rare occasions that we have guests remained untouched, so I made my way down to the living room. Empty. I called out her name, getting no reply. I had to try to recall what day it was, but this made no real difference. My wife had never been a morning person, and I could not remember a time she was out of bed, let alone the house, at this time in the morning. Something was wrong, of this I had no doubt.

I raced back up the stairs, grabbing my phone and dialling her number. The ringing on my phone coincided with a vibrating sound from her side of the bed. She never went anywhere without her mobile, and this revelation set off a fresh burst of panic within me. *What do I do?* I wondered, genuinely clueless. *The police won't be interested as she can't have been gone more than a couple of hours.* I racked my brain, trying to think of anywhere she could be but came up with nothing. There was nowhere that my wife would logically be before 7am, except in bed.

I threw on some clothes so that I could check outside to see if her car was still parked along the street, but I froze when I got to the front door. It was locked, with my keys in the lock, on the *inside,* just as it had been last night. Short of crawling through a window, there was no other way out of the house. The back door was never used, and so had piles of boxes stacked in front of it which had lived there since we had moved in. I checked, but they appeared to be undisturbed. The only other explanation was that she was still in the house.

I could feel tears welling in my eyes now, fearing the worst. She would have answered me if she could, which meant something was terribly wrong. I ran room to room, finding each one empty. Out of ideas, I went back to my plan to see if her car was still there. Sure enough, it sat in the space it had occupied for the last few days. I found her bag in the living room, which had also been left behind, containing her purse and keys. It was as if she had simply vanished. Having no other alternative, I called the police. I explained that she was missing, and yes, I understood that it had not been for very long. It was as I was detailing the mysterious knock at the door, the fact that the house was locked from the inside, and that she had left everything behind, I heard her voice. In a state of utter confusion, I hung up on the police call handler, and ran back up the stairs. Stretching her arms as she woke, lay my wife. Looking at her then, it was as if she had been there all along, but that could not have been.

"Where were you?" I demanded, fighting back tears. She looked confused.

"What are you talking about? I've literally just woken up."

"No..." I began, faltering a little,

37

beginning to doubt my own my mind. "I got up and you weren't here. I looked everywhere, even outside to see if your car had moved. I was calling you."

"If I didn't answer it was because I was asleep," she replied, starting to sound annoyed. "Perhaps you were having another dream? But don't worry, I'm right here."

"I'm taking the day off," I told her, changing the subject a little. "I don't feel right, and I think I need some rest. What are you doing today?"

"Nothing planned. Maybe we could just chill out, watch some TV, or something? You could have a nap on the sofa," she offered.

"That sounds nice," I replied, smiling weakly. "Let's do that. Bring the duvet down to the living room, and I'll find something to watch."

I made my way to the kitchen to make coffee, debating whether to make an appointment with the doctor, not noticing that one of the kitchen knives was missing from the block.

*Thursday evening*

The day went by in a blur, as I dozed between episodes of some fantasy drama that my wife had put on the television. My short naps were fitful, causing me to awaken in a panic but with no recollection of the details. I drifted off once more after dinner, at around 7pm, and slept for almost three hours. It was dark in the living room when I woke - the television was off and so was the lamp that my wife would sit beside to read. I called her name, but there was no response. I reached down the side of the sofa to find the switch for the lamp on my side of the room and flicked it on. The darkness was shattered by the glow, revealing a sight even worse than those which had come to me in my nightmares. On the opposite sofa sat my wife, head slumped forward, wrists cut by the knife which had landed at her feet. Between the two of us loomed the dark silhouette that I thought I had seen a few nights beforehand, and even in the light it appeared as a solid mass of blackness. The bulb in the lamp exploded after less than a second, just enough time for me to take in the horror of what I had seen. I tried to stand, but my legs gave out beneath me. I knew it was too late by this point, as I waited on the floor for the inevitable to come. Only it didn't. There was no attack on me, no sound or movement from the shadow. I pulled myself along the floor to the other lamp, cautiously flicking it on, expecting this bulb to shatter as well but it did not.

Light flooded on to the gruesome scene, and I reached for her, hoping it wasn't too late. I placed my hands over the wounds on her wrists in a futile attempt to stop the bleeding, but any chance of saving her had long since passed. I broke down in howling sobs, my head in her lap. When I had regained a little composure, I once again tried to stand, spotting the scrap of paper beside her. I unfolded it, trembling, terrified of what it would say. As I read the words over and over, I knew it was too late for me, also.

*I had to, I'm sorry. You're marked. They wanted me to kill you, but I wouldn't do it. I love you too much.*

## Riddles & Rewards

## PART 1 - SOMETHING FOR NOTHING

Darren didn't have a job, as such. He put this down to having, what he chose to call, a 'flighty' personality. He viewed his inability to stick with one thing as some romantic, free-spirited trait rather than mere procrastination or, heaven forbid, simple laziness. And this would have been perfectly fine had he had no responsibilities, but a long-term girlfriend and a toddler who was soon to be an older sibling certainly meant that he had some duties to adhere to. "It's time to grow up a bit", he had been told. If she had been completely honest, his girlfriend, Nell, had no objections to him only making tiny amounts of money, here and there, as it meant that he was their child's primary carer. She was free to work a more productive routine and took on the role as the breadwinner in their small, young family. However, maternity pay was pitiful in comparison to her usual income, and now he needed to step up, to be the man at last.

No one ever accused him outright of laziness; poor judgment seemed a more apt description of his work ethics. In between the part-time employments, which rarely lasted more than a fortnight, his focus was always to make money in one way or another. It had taken a stern ultimatum several months earlier for him to accept that on-line gambling and scratch cards were not a way to ensure an income and had, unsurprisingly, pushed them further into the red. Similar experiences had come along in the form of various pyramid schemes, which had ended up costing more than they had made, along with various other Internet-based plans, which anyone with a modicum of sense could see were a scam.

Then there were the competitions. To begin with it was magazines, trashy gossip ones, and the far too easy puzzles with huge cash prizes. Hundreds of entries were sent by post, the cost of mailing becoming a noticeable amount of money from their already stretched budget.

"You know they make those things so simple so that loads of people enter, right?" Nell had stated, as if it was the most obvious thing in the world. Perhaps it was obvious to everyone else, but the thought had never crossed Darren's mind; he was just pleased with himself for being able to complete the puzzles. Now she had made him feel stupid, but he could not formulate any reasonable defense as he was yet to win any cash prizes. "Surely if I enter enough competitions, I will win eventually." And he did. The following week he won a brand-new toaster. This was the result of many hours 'work' spent in a forum, the thread being entitled 'Making a living from competitions'. The premise was simple enough; users would post links to online competitions, only those which were free to enter, and usually with the answer to any question attached. With an extra email address set up to absorb the inevitable amount of spam from the prize-offering businesses, he set to work. In the second week, he won a voucher for a ten percent discount at a clothing store online as well as a children's watch.

"Cash would have been much more useful," he had been told, as Nell scanned their kitchen cupboards for something to snack on, the sparseness inside of them worrying her far more than she would let on.

"The cash prizes are a lot harder to get, but it's just a matter of time," he assured her. "And anything that we win and don't need can be sold easily enough." The number of available competitions, from sites around the world, was incredible. It filled his days and, as any cash pay outs continued to elude him, he began to work late into the evenings. Their second baby was due in three weeks, so really it could come at any time, and they just needed that one big prize to see them through.

Desperation had begun to sink in; time was running out. He had stopped even looking at what the prizes were some time ago, feverishly entering every possible challenge. And then it happened. Scrolling through pages of emails from the previous day's entries, he spotted one with 'congratulations' in the subject line. It made no mention of a cash prize, and it did not even seem to make sense as to what was actually being offered. The email read;

*Dear Sir,*

*Thank you for your entry. We are delighted to inform you that you are one of a small group of winners, randomly selected to take part in our mystery adventure. Should you wish to opt out then simply reply to this message with 'OPT OUT' in the subject line. Alternatively, if you are willing to seize this opportunity, respond with 'I'M IN!'. If you choose the latter, you will receive the first riddle within 24 hours.*

*Best wishes, and good luck!*
*Riddles & Rewards*

It was intriguing of course, so there was very little to think about. 'I'M IN!' "If it's not a cash prize, she won't want to know," Darren told himself, debating whether or not to mention this partial success to Nell. He began to daydream about what would actually be coming his way. It would not be long before he found out, and soon after that he would begin to realize the danger that he was in, with no foreseeable escape.

## PART 2 - THE RIDDLE

It arrived in less than twenty-four hours as promised. A little over fourteen hours, in fact. A matte black envelope landed on his doormat, silver script on the front which read R&R. Simple and elegant in appearance but enough to give Darren a chill. There was nothing more on the envelope. He thought hard as he stared at the silver font, desperately trying to recall if he had provided his address on any entries, virtually certain that he had not. He could fob off this notion, assuming that he simply must have divulged the information at some point, and perhaps he had. More worrying, however, was the lack of a stamp or any postage marks thus indicating hand delivery. "So, I must have put an address in, and it must be a local company," he optimistically told himself, gently prying the envelope open. The card inside was of the same shade of black as the envelope, the text in identical silver;

*You are one of six finalists. Think of this as a treasure hunt of sorts. Overleaf you will find the first clue, the easiest one of five tasks in total. Once you have solved the riddle and completed the initial assignment you must send photographic evidence to the email address used previously. The last contestant to respond to each of the tasks will be eliminated, leaving two of you to go head-to-head for the grand prize. Please note that failure to complete the tasks, as well as being the last to do so, will result in elimination and this carries a forfeit. Discussion of the challenge with any other person, by any means, will cause you to be removed from the experience, and a penalty will be given. Be brave and have fun!*

It was exciting, in a way, almost like a film. Everything about it felt mysterious but with an air of elegance, suggesting to Darren that there could be a prize worth claiming at the end of this. The indication of some kind of forfeit was a little unsettling, particularly as no details had been given, but it appeared that he had to, at least, try to win. Nervously, Darren turned the card over to study the same silver type, hoping that it would not be too cryptic for him to solve.

*1. I begin with T, I end with T, and I have T in me. What am I?*

And that was all that it said. Now he was no genius, of this he was well aware, but the first riddle had proven to be straight forward enough. What was not obvious, however, was what to do with the answer. Hurriedly, he opened his laptop and responded to the previous day's email, hoping that the other contestants had not found their envelopes before him. Unable to think of anything further to write, he sent the email with only the word 'teapot' in the subject line and waited for a response. The reply came through almost immediately;

*That is correct. We require you to attach a photograph of a teapot that you own, smashed onto your kitchen floor. You are currently the fifth respondent. Tick Tock.*

Without thinking, he pulled a teapot from the back of a kitchen cupboard and hurled it to the floor, shattering the red and white china. He photographed it, as ordered, and attached it to his reply.

Again, another email came through immediately, this time advising him of his success in reaching the next stage. He was to await further instructions.

Pregnancy had made Nell irritable at the best of times and the sound of crashing china had not helped matters. She came storming into the kitchen, looking not only angry but also bewildered by the mess that she was faced with.

"It slipped. I was going to make a pot for you," he explained, frantically stuffing the black envelope into his back pocket. She hadn't believed him, not uttering a word, just glaring as she struggled to crouch down and begin clearing up after him, the way that she always did. He swept up what he could, whilst she picked up the larger pieces, endeavoring to clear it before any shards found their way into Katie's toddler-sized feet. The front of the teapot, the part with the spout, had come off as one quite large piece. It was as Nell retrieved this from the linoleum behind the bin that something caught her eye. Something small and silver, like a charm. She looked at it with a puzzled expression, unable to fathom where it could have come from.

"What's this?" she asked, holding the short silver chain with silver letters hanging from it. Darren just stared, his face whitening, his heart starting to beat a little faster as he tried to process what was right in front of him, his eyes now transfixed on the letters R&R.

## PART 3 - RING RING

Fear had made itself known and, in the space of only a few moments, the sense of mystery and intrigue became something far more sinister. The hand-delivered envelope, the threat of penalties and forfeits, and now this silver charm, sparkling in his lover's hand. R&R. It made no sense for it to be in the teapot, for whoever was running this to not only know where he lived, but to have been *inside* his house. "If these are the lengths that they are willing to go to, I dread to think what the penalty for failure would be," he muttered. There was a prize to be won, however, and even without knowledge of what this prize may be, there seemed little point in quitting just yet.

There was no time to think things through as the awkward silence was interrupted with the shrill ringing of Darren's mobile telephone. The display indicated that it was a private number calling and, despite receiving these types of call quite often (usually from debt collectors), there was no doubt who this would be. He couldn't tell if Nell had detected any sign of fear on his face or not; she just looked angry and puzzled due to the teapot and the silver charm. The phone continued to ring, and he simply stared at the screen, his mind blank as if having forgotten how to answer it.

"Answer your bloody phone," she told him.

"Hello?" Darren said, barely audibly, as he slid the answer button across to green. The voice which came from the other end sounded robotic, automated. Not as though someone was attempting to disguise their voice, but the way that it sounds when a computer reads a piece of text aloud.

*"Welcome to round two. We require an emailed photograph of either one of the following two items. Pay attention as this message will not be repeated. A smashed car window or a smashed shop window. Before and after pictures must be provided. Hurry, and best of luck."*

It was only mid-morning, so the challenge brought with it a huge amount of risk. "I can't do that. I'll get caught." To Nell's complete surprise, Darren took off out of the house, running down the empty street, trying to formulate a plan. *What if I don't do it? What will happen?* Despite all logical thoughts telling him not to carry on, he felt as though he were on autopilot. "Smashing a shop window is not going to happen, there will be people everywhere," he told himself. If he had owned a car then, at least, it would have been possible to go down that route, as stupid as it may have been. Conscious of needing to respond before the other contestants, he raced along the river to a small car park and found only four vehicles there, with no one in sight. Ignoring the BMW, the Mercedes and the builder's van, he studied the beat-up Vauxhall Corsa. It was blue, mostly, with one red door. One hubcap was missing. Inside was a mess of soda cans, food wrappers, and the seats appeared to be covered in animal hair of some kind. He snapped a photograph of the car from the driver's side before picking up a large stone from the nearby pavement. Once he had checked that the coast was clear, he hurled the stone at the driver's window. The front seats became littered with cube-shaped pieces of safety glass, the stone now resting on the passenger seat. In pure panic, he fumbled for his phone to capture the second image

51

and ran, full pelt, towards home. He did not dare to look back in case he had been seen. He thought that he had heard a shout, but it was unclear over the sound of his quickened breathing.

Afraid of facing anyone at home, Darren ducked down the alley which led behind the street he lived on, emailing the photographs, as requested. There was no immediate reply this time, and he made his way back to the house, trying hard to think of an explanation to give Nell. "I can't tell her too much," he mumbled, not wanting disqualification, especially after his act of vandalism. "But if this is only the second stage, what will I be expected to do next? What will the last stage be, if I make it that far?"

As he entered the house, he found Nell still in the kitchen, a mug of tea in one hand. She looked distressed, presumably because of his behaviour; after all, it wasn't every day that he would smash a teapot and run out of the house following a mysterious phone call.

"A package came for you," she told him. He gazed at the kitchen table, studying the black box with the silver font on top.

"Who brought that?" he asked her.

"I don't know, a courier or something I guess. He just said it was for you. Those letters on it, R&R, they're the same as the ones in the teapot. Where are they from?" She didn't sound angry, but there was an air of suspicion in her tone, as though he was keeping something from her.

"It's just some competition prize, must be from the same company," he told her, trying to dismiss any concerns. Gingerly, he lifted the box, finding it much heavier than he had anticipated. It slid open from one end, like a box you would get a decent pen in. Inside was black silk, which cradled the item, an item he had certainly not expected.

"Well, that's not a great prize, but it is a nice box," she told him, rather unimpressed as usual, and made her way upstairs. The item itself was not of concern to him, however, it was whatever he was supposed to do with it that frightened him. Removing it from the box, Darren paced his kitchen awaiting further instructions and gripping the hammer firmly.

PART 4 - BLOODSHED

It felt like forever as he continued to pace the kitchen, hammer in hand, waiting for the next set of instructions to arrive. He presumed that he was successful in his second assignment, due to the delivery of the black box. It seemed unlikely that his next task would be any less dangerous than criminal damage, and Darren struggled to come up with a possible use for the hammer which did not involve anything illegal. To make matters worse, he had an overwhelming inclination that he was being watched. Thus far, he did his best to remain calm, not to panic. His composure was starting to fade though, a sense of terror gripping him as he realized that he was trapped in this game, for want of a better word. He had to choose between playing along or bailing out, and the consequence for simply quitting may be dire. There was still no word from the puppet masters. Nell looked startled as Darren rushed into the bedroom, hammer clutched tightly in his right hand.

"I need you to leave for a while," he told her, trying to hide the panic that had crept into his voice. "Take Katie and go somewhere, anywhere. I'll call you later to explain." Nell didn't want to go anywhere, and she made this very clear to him; certainly not without an explanation. Nevertheless, he could not provide an honest one, for fear of forfeiture. He was also unable to come up with a convincing lie, simply stating that he would call her later, and that she really needed to go. His eyes were wild, he appeared jittery, hammer in hand, and so, upon realizing that something was really wrong, she made her way out of the house, Katie clinging on to one arm and an overnight bag on the other.

He hated to frighten her like this, but he was just as afraid, if not more. She just had to trust him while he figured out what was going on. He sat, staring at his phone, waiting for some contact. The handle of the hammer had begun to feel slippery in his hands, which by now had become clammy with nerves. Then it came; the shrill ringing of another telephone call. Again, he answered cautiously, only to be greeted with a second automated message.

*"Welcome to round three. For successful completion, this time we require an emailed video of either one of the following two tasks. Pay attention as this message will not be repeated. Option one: Use the hammer and nail provided to fully pierce your right hand. Option 2: Use the hammer and nail provided to fully pierce the hand of someone else. Hurry, and best of luck."*

"What fucking nail?" he thought, grabbing the box from the kitchen table. Sure enough, among the black silk, there was a silver nail, approximately three inches long. "Option two is not going to happen! Not that Option one is particularly tempting either." Darren was becoming fed up with his lack of courage, either to go through with it or to just say no. He felt foolish, wondering if there really was a penalty for non-compliance. "The prize had better be worth all this," he told himself, too afraid not to carry on. "Why had the right hand been specified? Did they somehow know that I'm right-handed or was it an assumption?" Either way, it made the logistics of the act quite challenging. He would have to swing the hammer with his weaker, less efficient hand. It also left him no 'spare' hand with which to record the self-injury.

Viewing it as an act in which he had no choice, Darren quickly set to work and grabbed the first aid box from the kitchen cupboard, placing it down open on the work top. He grabbed the thickest of a set of wooden chopping boards to rest his hand on, hopefully meaning that he could avoid damaging the work surface itself. With some difficulty, he managed to prop his mobile phone up so that it was in the correct position to record the gruesome act, pressing the record button. "Don't over think it," he told himself, positioning the nail above the fleshy part between thumb and forefinger. "This is impossible," he realized, positioning the nail with his left hand and thus, being unable to hold the hammer. Without any further contemplation, he used his left hand to push the nail into the flesh, just far enough for it to stand on its own. It was agonizing, a sharp bolt of pain shooting from the wound up the inside of his entire right arm. He grabbed the hammer, desperately wanting the pain to stop, keen to have the job done so that he could tend to the injury. As he swung the hammer, the nail toppled out of its hole which was now well lubricated with thick, crimson liquid. The hammer was already in motion, and he could not stop it before it crashed down, causing a sickening, crunching sound. He let out a scream, not only from the searing pain but also from anger, a loss of temper. Frantically he pushed the nail back into the opening and tried again, the hammer now slippery with blood. It took three strikes for the nail to push far enough through, the tip finally having entered the chopping board beneath. Prising his hand free of the board, eye's watering, head feeling light, Darren grabbed his phone to ensure that the whole gory affair had been captured.

With his left hand, he quickly attached

the file to another email and sent it away into the ether. He stood, pale faced, dripping blood onto the linoleum and surveyed the mess around him. As quickly as he could bear, and looking away, he yanked the nail from his hand, causing a spurt of blood to arc across his wrist. It frightened him, causing him to wonder if he had hit a vein. He managed to squeeze a generous amount of antiseptic cream into the hole and began wrapping it with a length of bandage. As soon as the dressing touched his skin it became saturated in red liquid. By the time he had managed to stop the bleeding from showing through, the dressing had more than doubled the size of his hand.

Feeling weak, Darren slumped to the ground, his back resting against one leg of the oak dining table. There were pools of blood across the work top which ran down cupboard doors and dripped, slowly, on to the kitchen floor. The chopping board looked as though it belonged in a butcher's shop, the grain of the wood soaked in deep red. Loss of blood and the shock of what he had done caused his eyes to close. "I must stay awake," he told himself to no avail as blackness absorbed him, and he lost consciousness.

# PART 5 - THE PIG

He wasn't out for long, the throbbing of his hand having woken Darren up in a panic. From his position on the floor, he had managed to grab his phone from the kitchen work-top, wiped off a small dot of blood from the underside, and checked for updates but there were none. He thought he had heard his doorbell as he came around but was unsure, barely conscious at the time. He felt dizzy when trying to stand but needed to get to the bathroom, a strong desire to both urinate and vomit having come over him. He did his best to suppress the nausea, opting to empty his bladder from a seated position in order to avoid falling. Then the doorbell went again. The stream of urine seemed unending, and he knew he could not make it to the door speedily. Regardless of this, there was no-one that he wished to greet in his current state. Anyone he knew would undoubtedly want explanations as to why the kitchen looked like a scene from a horror film. If it wasn't anyone that he knew, then there was a good chance it would be the next stage in this game, and he had no intention of playing any longer.

The hammer and nail had been stupid, he knew that, but he had misjudged just how painful and messy it would be. There had been a steep escalation in the rounds, and he was certain that he could not handle whatever was coming next. "It's time to bail out," he decided, terrified that this was unlikely to still be an option. The doorbell rang again; whoever was there was not giving up easily. From the living room window, he pulled the edge of the curtain aside a little to see who was calling but there was no-one there. All that Darren could see was a small, black, cardboard gift bag hanging from the brass door handle.

Using his left hand, he carefully opened the front door just enough to reach the bag, quickly closing it again once the item had been retrieved. The bag bore the silver font which had adorned all the items so far, and inside he found two vials of liquid, identical in appearance except for their small labels; A & B. His first thought was that one would be poison and the other water, a gamble with his life perhaps. He placed the gift bag on to his kitchen table, alongside the previous box, and the now blood-stained hammer. "Quite a collection of prizes," he said aloud, reaching for his phone to find the details of round four. He had already told himself that he would not be playing any longer but was unsure how to get this message across other than by simply not corresponding any further. It was not long, however, before he made contact.

Once again, the phone rang but this time it did not show as a private number calling; rather it was the request for a video call. As he accepted the call, his eyes met with a man dressed in a black suit, expensive looking. His shirt was white and crisp, his thin, black tie bearing the now all too familiar logo of R&R. It did not come as a surprise that the man's face was hidden, a rubber pig mask fully concealing any areas of skin. A small microphone from within the mask ensured that he could be clearly heard as he spoke.

*"Good afternoon. In the two vials, you will find two different liquids. One is sodium thiopental, commonly known as truth serum. The other is a potent psychoactive drug similar to LSD. You must choose between the two, now."*

Darren had assumed that the video message was pre-recorded so it came as a surprise when the man behind the pig mask continued to stare at him, awaiting an answer.

"You can hear me?" Darren asked.

"Of course," came the reply. "Now you must choose a vial and let me see you drink it."

"No, I'm not playing any more. This whole thing is fucking sick." Darren retorted.

"I'm afraid that is no longer an option," came the voice from within the pig mask, as he continued to wait. Standing in his kitchen, looking at two vials of liquid which he had no intention of consuming, hand throbbing, Darren began to tremble. He was more frightened than he had ever been before, terrified of the consequences of his actions, regretting ever getting involved with those damned competitions. "Why didn't I just get a normal job?" he asked the empty house. *Fuck this!* Darren thought, ending the video call. There was a momentary silence, before it was quickly shattered by the sound of the doorbell once again, causing him to jump and drop his phone. Creeping as quietly as he could manage towards the front door, he flicked the second lock across and moved to the curtain to try to ascertain who was there. Was this going to be the penalty that he had to face? Panic turned to relief as he saw a police officer stood on his doorstep, aware that he was likely to be coming about the damage to the car. Darren could confess to that, explain what had been happening, maybe get some help. He fumbled with the locks and allowed the officer entry to his home.

The officer asked about the hand injury, explaining that he was there to investigate a complaint of criminal damage to a car. Darren explained everything, as honestly as he could, realizing how insane it all sounded. The policeman's presence was hugely reassuring though, taking the edge from the fear that he had been feeling.

"And you told him that you wouldn't be taking part any longer?" the officer asked.

"Yes, that's right," Darren replied.

"And how did he respond to this? The man whom you say was wearing a pig mask."

"He said that it wasn't an option, I don't know what he meant."

"Maybe he meant that you had to drink from one of the vials, whether you wanted to or not."

"Well, yes, perhaps, but they can't make me. Not unless they're planning on coming here and forcing me to."

"I'd say that was exactly what they are planning," the officer suggested, and before he had a chance to do anything, Darren felt a sharp scratch on his neck as a syringe was jabbed into it.

## PART 6 - ALTERED REALITY

Darren had taken enough recreational drugs in the past to know what the effects of LSD were like. Knowing what he had been given certainly helped, but the dose was much higher than anything that he had experienced before. The police officer, or at least the man claiming to be one, was still stood in the living room, his face contorted into a screaming expression, eyes bulging, mouth open wider than was physically possible. He looked terrifying and as Darren stared at the horror before him, he had to remind himself that it was only the drugs, and that it would pass. "Just stay still, ride it out," he told himself. Closing his eyes made no difference, images continuing to float around inside his closed eyelids. Scenes of blood-soaked rooms, swirling colours, deformed and ghastly faces. The sights before his eyes were moving quickly, changing from one image to another, none of them pleasant. He was of the opinion that psychoactive drugs merely enhanced the feelings the user had when taking them, meaning that the fear he had already been experiencing had been enhanced to an unbearable level.

The policeman's face and body kept shifting, his arms becoming longer and shorter, his eyes changing between black and red. It was unclear if anything was being said as there was just a muffled sound. When trying to stand, Darren's legs felt too heavy to lift and as he looked down at them, trying to find the cause of the problem, he came close to vomiting. Through his drug-induced gaze, his feet appeared bare, a silver nail piercing every single toe, through the centre of the toenail. The toenails were cracked, shattered pieces of keratin pointing in all directions. Blood soaked his feet and formed a puddle beneath them, slippery and warm under his soles.

"It's just the acid," he repeated to himself, over and over again. "If it was real, then I would have felt it."

Out of nowhere, his face began to itch. It itched all over, from his forehead down to his neck. He went to pull his hands to his face only to discover that they, too, were immovable. Both hands felt as one behind his back; he was unable to separate them. Pulling them as far as he could to one side he tried to see what held them together. There was nothing binding them, no handcuffs, no rope or duct tape. However, they no longer looked like hands, having taken on the form of two stumps, which had been welded together. This was unlike any acid trip he had experienced before and, even taking into account his mindset at the time of administration, Darren decided that this had to be a drug designed to cause these specific kinds of hallucinations. "But that is all they are, hallucinations."

The swirling images and distorted view of his living room had been shifting relentlessly, and he had no idea how long he had been in this state. It didn't feel like a long time, particularly, just a very unpleasant experience. As he stared at the figure before him, seemingly huger than before, it appeared to pull a dagger from its belt and move closer to him. He could only stare as the monster swung the blade toward his upper arm, causing a momentary chill to course through his entire body. It was as if the blade itself had become a cold, liquid metal, filling his veins. The icy sting spread across his chest and seemed to be counteracting the effects of the hallucinogen. In a state of shock and terror, he felt the itchiness of his face disappear. He watched in near disbelief as hands formed and shoes appeared on his feet, replacing the gruesome and violent bondage he had been so horrified by.

The chlorpromazine had taken effect

quickly, and despite never having used it before, he assumed that it was one of a range of anti-psychotic drugs often used to cut trips short. His mind was clearer, the trip ending rather abruptly, and now a level of exhaustion hit him hard. The police officer still towered above him, his face now looking much kinder.

*"You need a bit of a rest I think,"* he suggested. "Round five can wait for a few hours, then it'll all be over. I'm going to leave now and be on my way. I need you to stay sitting there until I'm gone, I don't want to have to hurt you, OK?"

Darren only wanted to sleep and was in no condition to put up any kind of a fight, slumping on to his side as soon as the cuffs were off.

"There's no rush, just take a break," he was told as the officer pointed to a box on the floor. It was about the size of a shoe box, in the consistent black with silver lettering. And with that, the officer made his exit, leaving Darren to drift into a nightmare-filled sleep on his sofa. "Just one more round," he murmured, as his eyes began closing. "Just one more."

PART 7 - MR. RANNIGAN

The descent from the trip was nowhere

near as bad as he had expected, the chlorpromazine counteracting the worst of the effects. The overwhelming tiredness was challenging though, his eyes feeling strained, every part of his body feeling heavy. He dragged himself from the sofa, rolling onto the cold floor, as he edged nearer to the final box. Whatever task lie within it, he knew he either had to try to complete it or have it forced upon him. Opening the box, he found two sealed black envelopes, as well as a black card featuring a list of instructions in silver text.

*Welcome to the fifth and final round. Upon completion of this last assignment, you will be rewarded with one of two available prizes, or a proportion of each. Inside each of the envelopes are details of each prize. You can choose to claim one prize in full, resulting in the disposal of the other. Alternatively, you can opt for some of one prize and some of the other. Please find your way to the address on the bottom of this card. Come alone or you will risk forfeiting both prizes. Well done for reaching this point!*

A rush of excitement came over him as he read the card, optimistically feeling that he had reached the end of the ordeal. The situation regarding collection of his prize felt off although he had little choice but to attend. He tore open the first envelope and found a Polaroid photo of a small, folding table. On the table was a stack of cash; a *lot* of cash. It appeared to be in bundles of one thousand pounds and there were around twenty of these. "Jackpot!" he said loudly. He then began tearing open the second, much thicker, envelope. It too contained Polaroid photographs; a bundle of them. As he flicked through them, he could feel his eyes beginning to well up, a mixture of sadness and fury filling his mind. The first picture was of his girlfriend, holding hands with their daughter. There was one of the three of them, taken at a nearby play park quite recently. Then there were another six or seven pictures only of Nell; they appeared to have been taken in rapid succession. As he turned to the next image, he could see her moving further into a state of undress, showing no sign of pregnancy. Then someone else appeared in the picture and it quickly became evident what the images showed. Every sordid detail of his girlfriend's unfaithfulness was presented there before him, but he could not stop himself from looking at each photograph. In the final, and most recent, picture she was dressed, heavily pregnant and restrained to a chair. Her mouth was gagged with a strip of duct tape, her eyes wild with fear. In the corner of the photograph Darren could make out the edge of the table containing the money, and it was clear that this last image was the situation, right now. "Are they really asking me to choose between her and the cash?" Darren wondered. "And how on earth can I take a portion of each prize?!"

Fearing for his own safety, he tucked a kitchen knife into the belt of his trousers, just in case. The address on the card was not far from his house, thankfully, and he could walk it in less than ten minutes. It was a storage facility, which wasn't surprising, due to the nature of the challenges thus far. As he approached the facility, he pulled the card from his back pocket to double-check the unit number. Thirty-four. A few moments later, he was stood in front of a corrugated metal door, the number thirty-four sprayed above it in red paint. He knocked cautiously, having no idea who he expected to answer. Nothing. Verifying the address for a third time, he knocked again, this time the door opening immediately, and he was taken aback to be greeted by an elderly man in another smart, black suit. On this occasion, there was no attempt to hide his face. Neither of them uttered a word as the elderly man pointed into the unit and closed the door behind them.

The room was cold and almost empty, concrete walls and floor completely bare of any decoration. The only items inside were two tables and a chair. On one table, as expected, was a stack of bank notes. On the chair, also as expected, Darren's heavily pregnant girlfriend was tied up and gagged but thankfully not showing any signs of injury. The extra table was the biggest cause for concern, however. On it featured an A4 sized black sheet of paper, with a list of items and prices, similar to a menu. Next to it lay a hacksaw, some rope and a backpack. Having received no explanation from the man who had greeted him, he began examining the menu, terror sinking in as he made his way down the list. Body parts and prices. This is what they meant by taking some of each prize. The first item on the list was a finger, deemed to be worth one thousand pounds.

"I don't understand," Darren said, fearing that he actually knew fully what was expected of him. Still the elderly man said nothing, instead dialling a number and handing him a telephone. The same automated voice came through, offering a little explanation.

*"This is the final round. You may leave with either the twenty thousand pounds or your partner. Should you wish to combine the prizes then you will see a list of body parts on the table. Each of these parts, we will purchase from you at the price stated. In case you were considering taking both prizes by force, Mr. Rannigan will rule out that option in just a moment."* As he turned towards Mr. Rannigan, he did indeed see that there was a very good reason why he could not just overpower him. Mr. Rannigan removed his suit jacket, shirt and tie, exposing his wrinkled, aging chest. Strapped firmly around him was some kind of explosive device, a detonator in his hand.

"You have ten minutes," Mr. Rannigan stated, watching calmly as his visitor racked his brain for a way out.

## PART 8 - FOR LOVE NOR MONEY

"If only she wasn't pregnant," he told himself. He knew that the 'right' decision was to take his girlfriend and unborn child home to safety. The thought that he had been through all of this for nothing was too much though. The suggestion seemed to be that, if he took all the money, then she would be gone, presumably killed. "There is no way I could let that happen but why rescue her if she's been unfaithful and the relationship may well be over? I'll end up with less than I had to begin with." He scanned the list again, trying to work out what he could get away with 'selling' without risking any harm to the baby, a baby whom he was now unsure was even his.

"I'm not leaving with no money," Darren whispered in her ear. "I'm sorry." Nell's eyes grew wider as she tried to shout something, but he did not want to remove the gag, afraid that she would convince him not to go through with it. Time was of the essence, and he had no intention of going home still broke and now apparently with a cheating girlfriend. A finger was worth a thousand pounds, but a whole hand was worth six thousand. "Surely that's a survivable injury, and six grand would see me through for a while."

He glanced toward the man wearing the explosives. "Seven minutes." Without any further thought, he grabbed the hacksaw, trying to block out the muffled sound of her screams. He set to work above her wrist, the hacksaw blade gliding through the flesh until it connected with bone. There was so much blood that he became terrified she may bleed out, but it was pointless stopping now. The blade was struggling to get through the bone, and he resorted to using his hands to snap what was left from the bloody stump. As it cracked off, Nell lost consciousness. Darren managed to place the hand on the table before vomiting onto the concrete floor. Stuffing six stacks of the bundled bank notes into the backpack, he looked back at Mr. Rannigan. "Five minutes," he was told.

With her being out cold, he assumed that one more item would be less difficult, the temptation of the money growing stronger the more that he looked at it. Scanning the menu, he weighed up his options, a foot perhaps, some teeth, an eye? The eye was worth four but there was no implement available for its removal. Ten thousand would be a good result, and she would have to adapt to her disfigurements; it wasn't as though he had much choice. The future of their relationship was looking more and more bleak, and his greed was taking over. As much as he hated to admit it, if she had not been pregnant, and now knowing about her infidelity, he may well have just left with the full twenty.

"Two minutes," came the voice from

across the room. Desperation kicked in, and it was now or never; he would have to deal with the aftermath when they got out of there. He lifted his unconscious girlfriend's head up and, looking away, dug the thumb and forefinger of his good hand into her eye socket. Trying not to vomit, he felt his way around to the back of the eyeball and yanked at it, freeing it from her skull. It remained attached by a red string of gore, and it took one further swift pull to release it completely.

Aware that time was getting away from him, he stuffed another four of the bundles into the backpack and set to work untying her. He cut her feet and arms free, removing the duct tape from across her face and lifted her limp, blood-drenched body from the chair. If he had been thinking, then he would have used the rope to make a tourniquet for the bleeding stump at the end of her arm, but he had been too focused on the cash. Her face was barely recognizable as blood gushed out of the sizable hole in it. As he made his way toward the exit, the old man looked at him with a grin.

Bursting through the door into the daylight, he carried the body as far as he could from the scene before calling for an ambulance. Despite having no idea how he could explain any of this, he knew that medical treatment could not be avoided. The ambulance arrived within minutes, and two burly paramedics strapped Nell to a stretcher and got her on board. He jumped in behind her and began explaining it was he who had caused her injuries, that she was also pregnant (despite this being rather obvious), and that he'd had no choice.

"There's always a choice," the paramedic told him. "You didn't have to take any of the money."

"I didn't say anything about money," Darren replied, his face full of fear, heart racing, shocked by R&R's apparent reach.

"Don't worry, you did well. The bosses have chosen you for a bonus round. We'll be there shortly."

# Teenage Kicks

I was excited by the thought of the trip. At seventeen, it was the first real chance to be away from my parents for a few days and hang out with my friends. Not that there was anything wrong with my parents, but I needed a little freedom. It had taken some work to persuade Mum and Dad to let me have three days away, and I must admit I wasn't entirely honest with them. But what seventeen-year-old hasn't lied to their parents? So, I told them I was going on a road trip with some friends. I explained that the Friday would be entirely spent travelling, Saturday we would see the sights in a city to the north, followed by a gig that our favourite band was playing, and then Sunday we would make our way home. All of this was true, so far.

Mum, understandably, wanted to know where we would be staying, who I was going with, and who would be driving. I gave her the details of the hostel as soon as it had been confirmed. However, I told her that I was going with Richie, Steven, and Kevin. In fact, I was going with Richie, Maria, and Eva. I knew my parents would have reservations about me staying overnight with a girl, despite me being plenty old enough, and I suppose I didn't want to risk being told I couldn't go. Looking back on those days now, I wish someone had talked me out of it. Perhaps if I hadn't been able to go, then none of them would have bothered, and we'd all still be hanging out together.

I had a part time job in a local shop at the time, and I was fortunate enough that my parents never asked me to contribute towards any bills, so whatever I earned was mine to use as I saw fit. That said, I was no good at saving and the trip was rather short notice, so I only had that week's pay to take. It was enough to cover my share of the fuel and the hostel, with a little left over for food, but I would owe Richie for the gig tickets still when we returned. I didn't know at the time, but this is something I wouldn't have to repay.

Richie's parents were well-off, more so than the rest of ours, anyway. So, naturally, he got the piss taken out of him with names like Richie Rich. It didn't seem to bother him, but he knew a few of our friends only hung around with him because he always had money on him. I genuinely liked the guy and was proud enough to pay my own way when I could, always paying back anything I borrowed as soon as I could. Having money did work wonders with the girls though, shallow as they seemed to be at that age. He had been with Maria for more than a year; a long time for people of that age, I guess. She had been born in Britain, but her parents were from South America originally. She was one of the prettiest girls at school, and Richie knew he was punching above his weight, but she seemed to honestly like him.

Eva, on the other hand, was not my girlfriend. There was something there, and there had been for a while, but nothing had ever happened between us. There was an unspoken agreement, as soon as we both agreed to go away together, that things may change in that department. What was to essentially be a three-day double-date would surely lead to the inevitable. Eva was not as pretty as Maria, at least not in body shape. She was dumpy but still carried the confidence to wear short dresses. She swore, and drank, like a sailor. She was both exciting and terrifying at the same time. If there was to be any coupling when we reached the hostel, I had no doubt who would make the first move.

Late Friday morning, Richie pulled up in his shiny red Vauxhall Astra to collect me. He had planned to pick up the girls before me, but I explained about the white lie I had told my parents. My bag had been thrown together the night before; a couple of changes of clothes, toiletries, a half bottle of vodka I had found in the kitchen cupboard, phone charger, and my wallet. I'd put a few condoms in my bag, hopeful that I would have a use for them, and not wanting to miss my chance by being unprepared.

"Morning Richie," my Dad said, approaching the car. "Where are the others? They live near you, don't they?" He eyed the back seat suspiciously. Richie didn't falter.

"Yeah, I went there first, but they weren't ready. They had chores to do, or something. I didn't want to get dragged in to helping, so I thought I'd come here." This seemed to satisfy my Dad.

"Well, you boys drive carefully. And no getting into any trouble." Dad turned to me, using a quieter voice so as not to embarrass me. "Please stay in touch. Let me know when you get there, and when you are on the way back, at the very least. Even if it's just a text. I love you."

"Love you too, Dad," I told him, giving him a quick hug and opening the boot of the car to throw in my bag. My Mum rushed from the house to wave me off, calling me over for a kiss, refusing to let me grow up. I made it quick, jumped in the passenger seat, and we were off.

"Time to get those bitches!" Richie announced. He meant it in jest; I knew he would never speak that way in front of the girls, so I laughed it off. "Did you get any booze?" he asked me, turning on to the street which Maria lived on.

"There is a little under half a bottle of vodka in my bag, but we'll need something to mix it with. What about you?"

"Oh yeah! An entire litre bottle of some fancy rum that was at the back of the drink's cabinet. I doubt anyone will notice, and if they do, I'll blame my brother." Richie stopped the car outside of Maria's terraced house and honked the horn. "She texted earlier to say her parents were already at work," he explained, as if he felt the need to justify not bothering to knock on the door. As Maria appeared, Richie climbed out of the car and opened the boot for her luggage. I tried to avert my gaze, but she was dressed as though she were heading to the beach; sandals, a bikini top, and hot-pants appeared to be all she had on. I waved feebly through the car window as she approached, and heard Richie complaining about the size of

81

Maria's suitcase. "Let's just hope Eva hasn't packed her entire wardrobe too," I heard him say. I could just make them out in the rear-view mirror, stealing a kiss while they had the chance.

"You're in the back," Richie told me, as he climbed back into the driver's seat. I knew better than to argue about it, and it would give me a chance to talk to Eva. My concern, I suppose, was how to keep the conversation going on a six-hour journey. My nerves started to build up as we entered Eva's street. The car stopped outside of the last house on the right-hand side, and no one moved. After an awkward moment, Richie turned to me and nodded towards the Eva's front door. With a sigh, I climbed out and made my way to the door.

Eva looked stunning, as though she had spent the entire morning getting ready. It only added to my nervousness, but there was a warm feeling inside as well, as I realised she had possibly made the extra effort for me. She was wearing a long summer dress, given extra girth by a petticoat underneath. She carried a small suitcase, much more sensible in size than the one Maria had dragged along.

"Hi," she said, biting her lip seductively as she greeted me. "Hope you're ready for this." I wasn't sure if she meant the trip or whether *this* meant her, but she was at the car before I could reply. Richie had hopped out to load her bag in the boot with the others, and I resumed my place in the back, quickly joined by Eva. It was time to head out of town, and there was an excited buzz in the car as we made our way, music blaring, windows down.

***

I was thankful for the volume of the music, as it made it almost impossible to be heard as we hurtled along duel carriageways, before reaching the first motorway. It would be a boring drive, Richie had warned, but the country route would have added an extra couple of hours. After three hours we were well over half way to our destination, and everyone agreed that food and a toilet break was much needed. Richie came off the motorway at the next exit, finding a spot in the busy services car park. There were a few fast-food outlets, a petrol station, and a pub. Richie was the only one of us who had already turned eighteen, and it was doubtful the rest of us would get served. On top of the fact that Richie was driving, we ruled out the option of grabbing some food at the pub if we couldn't get a proper drink. It would be far cheaper to get a burger and fries from one of the fast-food places, so that's what we did. We were all in high spirits, but thankful to have the chance to stretch our legs and maintain some conversation after the blaring music. Once we had all found our way to the restrooms, and ordered enough food to keep us going for the second leg of our journey, we found an empty table (the only one) and dived in. The food was average, and not all that warm, but we devoured it greedily. We talked nonsense for a while, bracing ourselves for the return to the road, slurping the last of our milkshakes.

"I'm going to try to have another piss before we go," I declared, waiting for a response from the others.

"Yeah, suppose it wouldn't hurt," Richie agreed, standing and walking with me to the gents. The girls showed no sign of moving, absorbed in a conversation about some movie they had seen recently. As we stood relieving ourselves, Richie spoke.

"The girls are looking good," he pointed out.

"Yep," I agreed.

"So, anything happening with you and Eva?"

"Nope. Well, not yet. Will see how it goes."

"You'll have plenty of time to see how it goes," Richie replied. "I'll be dragging Maria off somewhere private once we get to the hostel." He wore a smug grin, and rightly so, I thought. The way he looked at her, and the way he talked about her, weren't some macho bullshit about getting to bang the hottest girl in school. It was obvious he was in love with her, as much as anyone at that age could be in love.

We made our way back to the table and found that our seats had been taken by two guys. They looked older than us by a few years, but they were no bigger. The girls both looked uncomfortable, Maria quickly standing as we approached. The man who had positioned himself beside Maria reached for her, grabbing her by the wrist and telling her to sit back down. If I'm honest, I didn't know what to do. We saw the guys sitting there as we approached, and knew they were hitting on Eva and Maria, but to grab at them was a whole other thing. Richie saw the guy's hand move to his girlfriend, saw the petrified look on her face, and acted without much thought.

Before I could register what was happening, Richie's fist made contact with the side of the guy's head, knocking him to the floor. His friend rose to his defence, but Richie and I were either side of him. I shoved him forwards in time for Richie to react, grabbing the front of the guy's shirt and head-butting his nose, causing a sickening crunch and an outpouring of blood. The first man tried to stand but Richie kept him down with a full kick to the face. It was over in a few seconds, and we hastily made for the exit before there was any more trouble.

My heart was racing, and the adrenalin made me feel unsteady on my feet as I bundled into the back of the car with Eva. I felt sick, but Richie just wore this grin on his face, seeming to revel in the violence. None of us spoke as the car exited the parking area with a screech, and we were soon pulling out back on to the motorway.

"You okay?" I asked Eva, once the feeling of nausea had passed.

"Yeah," she said. "Thanks." She gave me a smile. "We could have handled those guys, you know?"

"Oh, I'm sure you could have," I told here, sincerely.

"Fucking pricks," Richie muttered. "They asked for it."

"They were staring at us as we arrived," Maria said. We all looked at her, not having noticed the men before the altercation. "Black Land Rover. They were leaning against it when we went into the restaurant."

"Well it's over now," I said, trying to reassure Maria more than anyone else. Richie responded by cranking up the stereo, shouting at the same time that we only had a couple more hours' drive ahead of us.

The journey was boring or felt more so following the excitement which had taken place during our rest stop. By the time we pulled in to the hostel car park, we were all keen to stretch our legs again, and I really wanted to get in a shower. It was hot and sticky in the car, even with the air conditioning blasting, and I needed to freshen up. We checked in and were shown to a dorm which slept eight people in four bunk beds.

"Are the other beds booked?" Maria asked. It was hopeful thinking that we may have the privacy of an actual hotel, but we were informed that, currently, they had no bookings for this room.

"That could change at any time, though," the receptionist told us. "We have people turn up at all hours, and I know the beds are filled for tomorrow night." She wasn't a friendly woman, but if I had to deal with partying teenagers and social misfits on a nightly basis, I probably wouldn't be all that welcoming. The place was cheap, and we only needed somewhere to sleep so I tried not to let it bother me. It was a far cry from the hotels my parents took us to on our occasional holidays, but this was supposed to be fun. We dumped our bags on a bed each, Richie and I taking one bunk bed, the girls taking another, provisionally, at least. I saw a sign for the bathrooms and showers, announcing that I would be heading there before anything else.

I had half-expected the showers to be an open, communal affair so was relieved to find individual cubicles. The water was hot, albeit not flowing with any real power, and I felt much more awake after I had finished. The others were already passing the bottle of rum about when I returned.

"What's the plan tonight, then?" I asked, aware that money was going to be needed for the following day.

"We were just talking about that," Richie replied. "I'm not bothered either way; we can go and try to get served in a pub somewhere or stay here, drink, and hope that we continue to have the room to ourselves." I looked about at the bare walls; the emptiness of the place made me think of what I assumed army barracks might look like. "There's a communal room, with a TV and some board games we could check out," he continued.

I was happy with that idea, and no one came up with any other suggestions, so we grabbed a couple of games from the communal room and returned to our dorm for some level of privacy. The communal area was empty, but it was still early and unlikely to stay that way.

We played a few games, the four of us sitting on the floor, passing the rum around and swigging from the bottle. In our hurry to leave the motorway services, we had forgotten to pick up any mixers for it, but it was smooth enough to manage. The cheap vodka in my bag would be another matter, so we had decided to keep that for the following day. We had all become quite relaxed by this point, enjoying the freedom of being away from home, and there was a sexual tension forming within our small group which almost reached breaking point when Maria suggested we play spin the bottle.

"Sounds fun," Eva slurred, "but I think a smoke first would be nice." My experience of drugs wasn't entirely non-existent, but on the couple of occasions that I had smoked weed before, it hadn't been all that pleasant. Nonetheless, peer pressure is a bitch, and I didn't want to embarrass myself. I caught Maria and Richie exchanging glances, as though able to communicate telepathically.

"We'll stay here," Richie stated, a mischievous grin on his face. "To keep an eye on the bags, yeah?" It wasn't remotely subtle, but Eva and I went with it, telling them we'd be back in ten minutes.

"Knock first, please," Maria said, siding up to Richie. I laughed, told her that I would knock but to watch out for the receptionist, and followed Eva out to the car park. We made our way along the side of the building, to not be too obvious, and Eva pulled an already rolled joint from her bag. We smoked in near silence, with me taking drags as small as possible without alerting Eva to the fact that I did not enjoy it. I checked my watch, satisfied that we had given Richie and Maria a little over ten minutes privacy and, with the joint gone, we turned to head back inside.

Eva took my hand, catching me off-guard as a pleasant tingle moved through my body. I couldn't help myself smiling, and held on to her, not looking her way. We crossed the car park, making our way back past the reception desk and towards our dorm. I was too wrapped up in the fact that Eva had taken my hand to pay much attention to anything else, not even noticing the imposing shape of a black Land Rover parked beside Richie's Vauxhall.

The idea of playing spin the bottle was better in theory than in reality. Richie had no issue with seeing his girlfriend kiss Eva when the opportunity arose, but when the bottle I had spun pointed to Maria, I knew he felt differently. He didn't voice it, perhaps feeling silly as the game had been her idea, but there was an unpleasant tension in the air at that moment.

"I think we should play something else," I suggested, much to the relief of the others.

"Aww, don't you want to kiss me?" Maria asked, feigning being hurt by my rejection.

"I'm not answering that," I stated, moving a hand on to Eva's leg.

"So, what shall we do now then?" Richie asked, stifling a yawn. Nobody had a suggestion to make, and it was decided that we would get to bed. To be honest, it was clear that Maria and Richie wanted to get to bed as they had unfinished business from earlier, but neither Eva or myself were quite ready to try to sleep whilst listening to our friends grunting nearby. Without explanation, Richie took his bag from the bunk we had claimed, and moved it over to Maria's, exchanging it for Eva's. I waited nervously to see if Eva was planning for us to share a bed, or if I needed to take the top bunk. She offered no clue, instead pulling out another joint from her bag.

"Anyone want to join me?" she asked. I didn't want to smoke any more but would have gone with her if no one else offered. I felt a little pang of relief when Maria offered to go.

"Girl time!" she announced, and the pair disappeared from the room.

"You got condoms?" Richie asked me, as soon as the girls were out of earshot.

"Yep," I confirmed, my nerves clearly evident. "Did you not get some action earlier?"

"We started to, but ten minutes wasn't long enough. We made a good start though," he told me with a smile. "This is going to be a good weekend!"

It was somewhat ironic that the words *good weekend* should be almost drowned out by a scream, but that is what happened. We couldn't tell immediately who the scream had come from but were certain that it was one of our companions. We launched ourselves out of the room, past the startled receptionist who had previously been engrossed in a trashy magazine, and out into the darkness of the car park. Eva was standing on the gravel, tears flowing freely, mascara running down her face leaving black trails.

"Where's Maria?" Richie demanded, his eyes darting around the car park. Eva pointed to the exit.

"They took her!" she sobbed. I stared at Eva, not following what was happening.

"Who took her? I don't understand," I said, as calmly as I could manage.

"The guys from earlier. In that black Land Rover. They came out of nowhere, one of them picked Maria up and threw her in the back of the car. The other one tried to drag me in, but I stuck my finger in his eye. I couldn't stop them." Eva broke down in tears and I felt as though I would vomit.

"Fuck!" Richie screamed. He raced into the hostel, telling the receptionist to call the police. I could make out the word's *girlfriend kidnapped* and *black Land Rover.* He must have gone to the dorm while I stood uselessly beside the crying Eva, as he returned with his car keys, anger glistening in his eyes.

"We need to wait for the cops," I told him. "You're way too pissed to be driving, you'll end up killing yourself." My words fell on deaf ears.

93

"If you want to stay then do what you want. They will be long gone by the time the cops get here, and anything could have happened to her by then. They only have a few minutes head start, so I have to try." I understood what he was saying, and it did make sense. I also felt the same level of anger towards these men, and the same fear as to what they had planned for Maria. Therefore, I got in the car, and told Eva to stay put.

"I want to come," Eva whined.

"Someone needs to describe the car to the police," I reminded her. "And give them a description of Maria. Did they go left or right?"

"Left," Eva replied. Leaning in closer, in order to be less likely to be heard by Richie, I told Eva to tell the police we had given chase, to tell them what car we were in, and that we have been drinking but had no choice. *Best to be honest,* I thought.

As soon as Eva stepped away from the car window, Richie threw the car into reverse, kicking up gravel. We sped out of the car park, turning left on to the quiet road, Richie hammering up the gears until he had pushed the Vauxhall to over ninety miles per hour. It was a long, straight road and it took only a few minutes before we could see tail-lights up ahead. We must have been a couple of hundred metres behind when we saw the shape of a large black car turn off to the right, its headlights moving up and down as it traversed a bumpy track. Richie hit the brakes, slowing the Vauxhall down enough that we would not miss the turning, flicking off his headlights as we turned.

The darkness enveloped us, preventing us from being able to see the track before us, and Richie crawled the car along slowly for a few minutes. The Land Rover was still in sight, coming to a stop just ahead, the shadow of a large barn looming nearby. Richie shut off the engine and moved to open his door. I grabbed his arm.

"Wait a minute," I told him, whispering. "They will see us coming. Call Eva, tell her where we are so she can send the police."

"You fucking call her," he replied angrily. "I'm going to get Maria." I quickly sent a text to Eva, telling her we had followed the car along a track to the right of the main road, and to send the police. Richie was already out of the car, closing the door as quietly as he could, and had begun sneaking towards the barn. Three silhouettes could be made out beside the car, and I opened my door to follow. I may not have been particularly tough, but I knew I needed to be there for my friends.

As I closed my door, I realised that we were blocking the trail, from this end at least. Fine if our plan was to keep the Land Rover from escaping, but it would also prevent the police getting any closer.

"Richie," I called, trying to keep the volume as low as possible. He turned to me just as a scream came from Maria, followed by a thud. We turned towards the barn and saw two men carrying Maria's unconscious body inside. Richie took off at full speed, with me following behind. Richie didn't hesitate in shoving the barn doors open, startling the two men inside. I was only a few seconds behind him and was able to see Maria lying on the dirty floor, one man holding her down at her shoulders while the other pulled her hot-pants down to her ankles; their intentions were all too obvious. Richie had lost his temper when Maria had been grabbed in the restaurant, but that was nothing compared to how he reacted at this point.

As he raced towards Maria, the two men leapt to their feet. Richie lunged, intending to hit the guy at Maria's ankles. I was only a couple of metres behind and it took me a second to understand what had happened.

Richie appeared to trip, only inches from making contact, and fell forwards onto the barn floor. He landed with a wet thud, groaning, blood pooling from beneath him. His attacker stood, a machete in hand, now dripping with crimson. I froze.

With very little thought, I ran. I knew my chance of escape was slim, and the thought of leaving my friends to die would rack me with guilt, but I was no match for two armed men. All I could hope was that the police were almost here and perhaps it wouldn't be too late. I turned on my heels, dashing into the darkness outside and back towards Richie's car. I knew they were coming; I could hear their footsteps pounding on the ground behind me. The car was in sight and I would have made it inside if the damn keys weren't still in Richie's pocket. Realising my error, I continued straight past the car, but I knew they were gaining on me. A second later the blow came, throwing me forward onto the gravel. Instinctively, I rolled on to my back and was greeted by a kick to my ribs. Machete guy pointed the shiny blade at my throat and told me to get up. Out of options, I found myself being led back to the barn. *What was taking the police so long to get here?* Pushing me through the door, I heard one of my attackers mutter the word *shit,* and saw that Maria was no longer on the ground, her shoes now the only evidence she had been there. Richie had not moved, and I could not detect the rise and fall of his chest. I knew then that he was gone.

"Find her!" machete guy yelled, causing the other man to run back out into the darkness. If he had been unarmed then there is a chance I could have taken him, but the weapon, coupled with the blow to the back of my head and the kicks I had received, did nothing for my confidence.

"You run, and I'll gut you like your friend," he snarled, and I had no doubt that he would go through with it. He kept a rough grip of my shoulder, pulling me about the barn until he found some rope which he used to bind my wrists and ankles. He pushed me to the floor, a bolt of pain shooting up from my coccyx as I landed. I wanted to speak, to ask why this was happening, but it seemed unnecessary. These guys were clearly psychotic; our altercation earlier in the day having sent them after us, hell-bent on revenge. All I could do was to try to stay alive long enough for the police to arrive and hope that Maria had made it to safety.

"We're going to enjoy that pretty bitch

when we find her," machete guy taunted. "And then you'll see what a mistake it was to fuck with us." I couldn't bring myself to look him in the eye, through fear largely, but I did notice a flash of movement behind him. It was silent, and fast, but it took me only a moment to register who it was. *She should have run,* I thought, shocked that she had remained deliberately. The soft padding of her bare feet on the barn floor only became perceptible as she came to within a foot of machete guy, and by that time she had driven a rusty pitch fork through him. He hadn't even had time to turn around, and I watched as his eyes widened, four prongs bursting from his chest. The fork in Maria's grip held him up for a moment, as the life gurgled from him, and she allowed him to drop to the floor as I pushed myself out of the way. Maria fumbled with my restraints, pulling me up from the ground.

"Keys," I mumbled, running over to Richie's corpse. I checked for a pulse, just to be certain, but to no avail. I took the keys from his pocket and grabbed Maria's hand. She had picked up the discarded machete, holding it firmly, still looking crazed with plans of vengeance.

"Just in case," she told me. I nodded, desperately hoping that we wouldn't need to use it. We ran as quickly as we could manage to the car, and I tossed the keys to Maria. Neither of us knew how to drive, but I didn't want the pressure of figuring it out at that moment. Starting it up and crunching the gears into reverse, we made our way back along the track, hitting every hole in the road. Maria fumbled with the levers, searching for the headlight switch. They came on in a blaze of brilliance, illuminating the shadow of a man running towards us.

"Oh fuck," she cried, trying to make the car go faster, but struggling to see where we were going. The car lunged back, dropping as one of the rear wheels went into a hole too big to pass over. The more Maria revved the engine, the more the wheels spun uselessly.

"We have to run," I shouted, opening my door before she could answer. I scrambled out, and round to Maria's side to help her but he had caught up with us. Thankfully, he didn't appear to be armed, but he was intent on hurting, possibly killing, us both. Maria had the driver's door open, one leg out, when he ran up and kicked the door as though to shut it. There was a crunch as Maria's calf shattered, and she let out a deafening howl. He dragged her out onto the track, fists and feet flying as

100

he bombarded her with a relentless attack. It was as though he wasn't paying any attention to me, seeing me as less of a threat than this girl, but it afforded me the opportunity to grab the machete from between the front seats.

I could just about make out Maria's face in between punches; a swollen bloody thing now unconscious, or worse. I had no choice and swung the blade into the man's neck. He yelped, turning around. Blood appeared to be gushing from the wound, but he was still standing so I swung again, two or three more times, until he dropped to the ground. He twitched for a moment, falling silent with his eyes still staring up at me. I moved to Maria, her pulse weak but still there, and picked her up. The car would be no use, and so I carried her, tears falling down my face, as far along the main road as I could manage.

The police finally arrived, having seen me at the side of the road. It was too late for Maria; she had taken her last breath as I struggled along the roadside, but I had so desperately wanted to get her back to the hostel. I told them what happened, as honestly as I could manage, but I was angry with them; angry they had taken so long to get here. They said they didn't know where to look, that we had only been gone for a little more than half an hour, that Eva had not passed on the message I told them I'd sent. I checked my phone, and the tears came faster. *Message failed.* Lack of signal, most likely.

My parents were called to collect me, but it was early morning by the time they arrived. Stupidly, I thought I'd be in trouble for the drinking and the presence of girls, but they weren't going to be telling me off after the ordeal we had been through. Eva's parents also arrived around the same time, and she hugged me goodbye. The memories of that night, and the gossip which was inevitably going to flow through school, led to me moving. I never saw or spoke to Eva again after that hug.

"You want to stay in a cabin in the woods? Have you never seen a horror movie?" Joanne asked me, her mouth curving upwards into a playful smile.

"It's not a cabin, it's a caravan. One of those static homes, and it looks really cosy," I told her. She may have been making jokes, but I was disappointed that she hadn't seemed as excited as I was. Our relationship was still in its infancy, just three wonderful months in. We were enjoying the excitement of spending time with each other, most of which was spent exploring one another's bodies, and for the first time ever I felt as though this relationship could be the one. "I just thought," I continued, "that it would be more relaxing than a hotel in the city."

"More secluded," she replied. "If I didn't know any better, I'd think you just wanted to ravish my body in the woods all weekend."

"Well..." I said, grinning. She knew what I planned for us to get up to, and the look in her eye suggested she was more than happy with that.

"So, what time Friday?" she asked.

"We can check in from 4pm, so I can

pick you up at 3?"

"Anything you want me to bring? Food? Something to do?"

"The owners are putting a welcome pack in the caravan, so there'll be tea, milk, eggs, and so on. Thought we'd take a few board games, and maybe bring a book?" I suggested.

"Okay, I'll find a few things to bring. And some alcohol."

"Of course!" I declared. "Booze and board games sounds great." Joanne kissed me goodbye and left to go home to pack. I reminded her she wouldn't need much, and it was two days until we left, but she insisted upon being organised. I knew I'd put off my own packing until an hour before leaving, but there really wasn't going to be much to take.

***

I pulled up outside of Joanne's apartment block just before 3pm on the Friday, as planned. My small suitcase was in the boot of my battered, old Ford Fiesta, and contained toiletries, a change of clothes, a bottle of rum and some cola to mix it with, my Kindle, a Monopoly set, and a Scrabble set. I honestly couldn't think of anything else to bring aside from the essentials like keys, wallet, phone, and phone charger. I pressed the buzzer beneath the number thirteen and was granted access without Joanne bothering to ask who was there.

"You ready?" I asked, excited to be going away for a few days.

"I think so," she stated, taking a final glance around the living room. "It's just this bag," she said, nodding towards a small holdall on the floor, "and that shopping bag". I peered inside the shopping bag, spotting some snacks, a bottle of gin, and plenty of tonic water. I picked up both her bags while she locked up, and we placed them in the boot of the car alongside my own case, before heading out on to the country roads.

"It's a lovely day," she said, gazing out of the window. She was right; it had stayed warm for what felt like months now, even as we hurtled through October. "How far is this place?"

"About an hour," I told her, glancing at the sat-nav. "Maybe a bit less if the traffic isn't so bad."

"You say it's just one caravan? Not like a park, or something?"

"Just the one, that I know of," I confirmed.

"So, do we go to the owner's place for

the keys?" she enquired.

"They have a lock-box on the side of the caravan apparently. There is a security code that came on an email when I booked it, so we can just let ourselves in."

"Sounds perfect," Joanne said, smiling at me.

\*\*\*

The country roads were virtually empty, and I would have managed to knock almost ten minutes off the estimated journey time if we'd been able to find the place more easily. The postcode which had been provided simply led to an unnamed road, more of a track than a road, in fact, and without any sign post to indicate the turning, we missed it. I continued along the road until I reached a roundabout and headed back in the direction the sat-nav was indicating, taking it more slowly. On our left were three turnings, only a few metres apart, so we took a guess and turned into the middle one.

"There!" Joanne squealed, startling me a little. I stopped the car, unsure of what she had seen, and looked across her. "There's a sign, but it's not much use down there." She was right; a small wooden board with spray-painted lettering declaring Rural Retreat lie propped against a small bush, with an arrow suggesting we follow the trail. My old Fiesta didn't seem to like navigating the huge holes in the ground, and I heard the underside of the car scrape against the earth on more than one occasion. The trail seemed to go on for miles, but we eventually pulled into a clearing where a much larger than expected caravan stood proudly.

From the quality of the signage, I had begun to worry that the caravan would be rather decrepit, but it looked spotless on the outside. I switched off the engine, glad to be able to stretch my legs as I climbed out and stood on the grass. Peaceful would have been an understatement. There was the sound of a few birds, but we were far enough away from the road to not hear any traffic, and it was evident that no other people were anywhere nearby.

"It's lovely," Joanne said, happily looking around at the trees which almost completely surrounded the caravan. I agreed, checking my email for the code to use in order to retrieve the keys. The lock-box was attached beside the door to the caravan, and I pulled back the cover to expose the keypad. I input the four-digit code and turned the latch, letting out a sigh of relief that it had opened without any difficulty. I unlocked the door to our weekend residence, and held it open for Joanne to enter first. I wanted to see what she made of the place, and the squeal of delight told me I had chosen well.

The caravan only had one bedroom, as it was intended as a romantic getaway, rather than for family breaks. This allowed for more living space, and the lounge area was well-equipped. Alongside a television, there was also a DVD player, with a stack of films to choose from. These were mostly romantic comedies, but we spotted a few classic horror movies in the pile as well. There was a huge corner sofa, with more than enough space for us to sprawl out across, and a small, but practical, kitchenette. I was bursting for the toilet when we arrived, so made my way there and was excited to see a rather deluxe-looking shower. Easily big enough for two, I thought, making plans in my head for later that night. Once we had unpacked, Joanne cracked open the gin she had bought, and filled two hi-ball glasses. We slumped on the sofa, enjoying the quiet, feeling perfectly happy. It was looking as though it would be a wonderful weekend.

"So, what do you want to do first? Or is that a silly question?" Joanne asked.

"I'm up for anything," I told her, my eyes

darting from her face to her cleavage and back again. "The shower looks big enough for two." Joanne stood up, making her way around the caravan and closing all the blinds.

"There isn't anyone about," I reminded her.

"I know, but I don't like the thought of some pervy dog-walker catching sight of us. Set up one of the games, and I'll be back in a minute." As I set up the Monopoly board, my mind wandered on to Joanne returning from the bedroom in some slinky nightdress, but that wasn't the case. When she did return, I can honestly say my heart skipped as I looked her up and down, now scantily clad in an erotic maid's outfit.

"Oh my," is all I could manage to say.

"Something wrong?" she asked, smirking at my reaction.

"Definitely nothing wrong," I replied, trying to finish setting out the game, grinning like a schoolboy. We never did finish the board game. Almost two hours into it, and half a bottle of gin later, our lust for one another took over and we ended up making love on the sofa. It was barely 7pm, so too early for sleep, and I suggested we watch a movie.

"I'll get sleepy if we watch TV," Joanne

said. "I've got my tarot cards, if you fancy a reading?" She had mentioned owning tarot cards not long after we met, but my cynicism and lack of real interest had meant she had never tried to actually get them out in front of me. I could see, however, that she was keen to show me. I agreed to let her perform a reading and told myself not to take the piss too much. Joanne disappeared to the bedroom to retrieve the cards, and we made a space on the sofa between us for her to lay them out. I must admit, I was quite drunk by this point, as well as physically exhausted from the rather frantic love-making, so I wasn't paying all that much attention to what I was being told. I tried my best to sound interested, but each card came with some generalised meaning which could be applied to anything. It was only as Joanne turned over the final card, I spotted a worried look on a face.

"What is it?" I asked, trying to take her concern seriously.

"Nothing," she muttered. "It doesn't matter."

"You look spooked," I pressed. "What did that card mean?"

"Well, you don't believe any of it, so just forget about it," she replied, almost angrily.

"Hey, I know it's something you're into, so I'm trying to be involved. Am I about to die, or something?"

"It is the Death card; the thirteenth trump I think it's called. But it doesn't necessarily mean actual, physical death."

"So, what does it mean?" I asked, trying to be patient.

"Well, it can mean death, either your own, or someone close to you. But more likely, it represents the end of something," she explained.

"Like what, losing my job?" I asked.

"Maybe. Or the end of a relationship." I could see a tear form in her eye as she said this, and there was no doubt she believed in the cards.

"You honestly have nothing to worry about there, I promise," I told her as I took her hands in mine. "I'm not going anywhere." Joanne gave me an unconvincing smile, before putting the cards away and making another drink. "So, if you don't fancy a movie, should we try to finish Monopoly? Or did you bring anything else?"

"Promise not to laugh," she told me. I stayed silent. "I brought a Ouija board too." I couldn't help myself and I let out a chuckle.

"So, let me get this straight. You said

that staying out here in the countryside was like the plot from a bad horror film, you got freaked out after reading Tarot cards, and now what, you want to speak to a ghost?" She couldn't deny that I was making sense.

"I thought it'd add to the spooky atmosphere out here, now that it's getting dark. You know being frightened is an aphrodisiac, right?"

"You in that outfit is an aphrodisiac," I told her, feeling ready to perform for her again. "Do you actually think Ouija boards work?"

"Probably not," she told me, and I was pleased with her answer. "But it could be a laugh."

"Fine," I said, certain that nothing would happen, and it'd be a quick activity. "On one condition." She cocked her head to the side, ran a hand across one breast, and whispered 'anything'. "We get in the shower afterward," I stated, trying to sound authoritative.

***

We cleared away the Monopoly set and sat back around the small dining table. Joanne placed the Ouija board on the table, resting the planchette in the centre.

I sipped at my drink while she read through the rules, which seemed to just be a few paragraphs to ensure the 'players' use the correct phrases.

"It says to make sure electronic devices are switched off, or at least out of sight. My phone is in the bedroom, but there wasn't any signal when we got here," she told me.

"I turned mine off a while ago, not wanting any interruptions," I replied. "What else does it say?"

"Don't play anywhere spooky, but it's too late for that. Respect any spirits you encounter and be happy so as to give off positive energies. Apparently, this reduces the chance of an encounter with a demon."

"Well, I'm pretty happy, so I'm sure we'll be fine. Just friendly ghosts, yeah?" She smiled, seeming to relax after her earlier upset with the Tarot cards. "So, how do we start?"

"Place a finger gently on the planchette," she ordered, placing one of her own fingers beside mine. Holding up the instruction sheet, she began to read from it. "Are there any spirits here who would be willing to talk to us?" There was silence. "I'll ask again, are there any spirits here who would like to communicate with us? We mean you no harm." Again, nothing. If truth be told, I felt a little foolish at that point, sat in silence in my boxers.

"I guess not, then," I mumbled. I could tell Joanne was a little disappointed, but I was relieved. My relief was to be short-lived. I pulled my hand away from the board just as the planchette shot across the board, undoubtedly pointing to YES. We looked at each other wide-eyed. "How did you do that?" I asked Joanne, suddenly afraid that perhaps it hadn't been her.

"I didn't do anything, I haven't even moved my hand," she told me, her voice trembling with a mixture of fear and excitement. Her hand was still hovering over the centre of the board, and I doubted that she had been able to move the planchette and get her hand back in place without me noticing.

"Yes what?" I questioned. "Yes, there's a spirit here?" I looked at Joanne as I asked this, but it was evident I was speaking to anyone, or anything, that was in that caravan with us. The planchette remained still. With fingers poised as described in the instruction guide, we continued to bombard whatever entity we thought was communicating with us. Who are you?

What's your name? How did you die? Nothing more happened, we began to doubt what we had seen, and the Ouija board was quickly discarded in favour of some sensual time in the shower.

*** 

Our evening had culminated in us moving our carnal act from the shower to the bedroom, and once our desires had been satisfied, we had fallen asleep naked in each other's arms. The gin had all gone, and we'd made a start on the rum as well, so it wasn't surprising that I woke up in need of the bathroom and a glass of water. I clambered out of bed, checking my watch to see that it was exactly 3am. It was also much colder than I had expected, and I shivered as I stood. Stepping into the hallway, I fumbled for the light switch, not entirely sure where it was located. When I found it, the light dazzled me, causing my eyes to close briefly. I took a couple of steps forward before trying to reopen them, and then I let out what could only be described as a shriek.

Every cupboard, every drawer, and every window were open. My initial thought was that we had been burgled, and was briefly relieved to recall that our phones, and what little cash we had with us, had been safely left in the bedroom. Joanne must have been awoken by my cry and startled me when her voice whispered in my ear, asking what was wrong. Her eyes looked over my shoulder and into the living area of the caravan, widening as she took in the scenes of disturbance. Before she could speak, every open door, drawer, and window slammed shut at the exact same time. This time we both screamed.

Darting back into the bedroom, we threw on clothes and chucked any belongings into our bags. We hadn't spoken any further, but both knew we had to leave, quickly. I pulled at the caravan door, finding it locked. Of course it's locked, I thought, remembering that I had locked us in as soon as we had arrived so as not to be disturbed by anyone. But I'm sure I left the key in the lock. The key was nowhere to be seen, and I frantically dashed about the caravan in search of it, panic causing my entire body to shake. Without any luck, I was left only with the bathroom to check, but I knew this would be pointless. It was as I glanced across the tiled floor that Joanne shouted.

"I've found it!" she called, her voice trembling. I approached her, standing as she was in the centre of the living room, gazing at one of the windows. Her face had turned an unnatural shade of grey, and the shaking in her hands had not relented. I looked, in the direction that she was staring in, and saw the impossible sight. The key was there, fixed against the window, but on the outside. I approached it, running my hand across the glass to be certain. It was definitely on the outside, and try as I might, the window which had recently been fully open now refused to move. There was no choice but to smash the window and make our escape.

Taking a frying pan from the kitchenette, I swung as hard as I could, expecting the glass to shatter noisily. I may as well have been using a newspaper, for all the good it did. We stood in silence for a moment, terrified, sweating despite the cold, hearts thumping in our chests. Then came a sound, almost imperceptible, but definitely there. A gentle squeak, as though something plastic were sliding across a smooth surface. Our heads turned toward the small table, shock setting in as we watched the planchette move across the board, slowly, deliberately. My gaze landed upon it as it moved from the letter E, so at first, I thought it was spelling out the name Edie. We watched in pure horror as the planchette drifted from one letter to another, becoming faster and faster, repeating that one, small word - die.

"What have we done?" I asked Joanne, now having no doubts about the power of the Ouija board. With determination, she leapt forward, grabbing the sheet of paper which detailed the instructions.

"There must be a way to stop it," she muttered, her eyes scanning through the rules. "Shit, we didn't say goodbye!"

"Goodbye to what?" I asked. "Nothing had happened; there was no one to say goodbye to."

"That doesn't matter. It says the most important part is to move the planchette to the goodbye point at the end, even if nothing appears to have happened, and this will end the connection with the spirit." Joanne reached for the planchette, attempting to stop it between the letters I and E, but screamed when her hand came into contact with the small, plastic-coated piece. She instinctively put her fingers to her mouth, sucking on the burnt and blistered tips. The planchette continued its horrific movement, and I moved towards Joanne. I held her, our faces buried in one another's shoulders, unwilling to stare at the board any longer. The sound of the planchette moving had reached an unbearable level and then, seemingly out of nowhere, there was silence. Cautiously, I moved my hand to the board, and found it to no longer be hot. I looked to the window, unable to see the key fixed to the outside of the glass.

"It must have fallen," I stated, the pounding in my chest refusing to slow as I feared we were trapped.

"We're not trapped," Joanne told me, pointing to the door. Sure enough, she was right; the key was now back where it should have been.

"That did just happen, right?" I asked, suddenly doubting my own sanity. Joanne showed me her injured fingers as evidence.

"I don't want to stay here," she said, and there was no disagreement from me. We loaded our things back into the car, (minus the Ouija board which we left where it was as no one had wanted to touch it), replaced the key in the lock-box, and headed down the track towards the main road. Neither of us spoke for almost half an hour, when Joanne broke the silence.

"You should have said goodbye," she told me. "But I'm glad you didn't." My tired brain took a moment to realise she wasn't making sense.

"I should have said goodbye? And you're glad about what? Glad we went through that?" I was almost angry at her.

"If you had said goodbye, I would have had to leave. But now I'm free." I took my eyes from the road to look her way, finding her staring at me, grinning. Even through the darkness within the car, I could see something was wrong with her eyes. I barely had a moment to consider this before she had grabbed the wheel and unclipped my seatbelt. The car flew off the road at sixty miles per hour, the tiny Fiesta crumpling as it made contact with a brick wall, and my final memory was a feeling of weightlessness as I was launched through the windshield to my death.

121

# Fossil Bluff

*Day One*

Will shielded his eyes from the glare as the aircraft descended towards Fossil Bluff. The sun was high in the sky, but it wouldn't be that way for long. The short Antarctica summer was coming to an end, but Will's trip was only beginning. Excitement mixed with nerves as the pilot lowered the wheels on the small plane. Will had foolishly read an article about the dangers of landing on ice-covered runways and couldn't stop himself from closing his eyes as the aircraft struggled to keep a straight course on the ground, only opening them again once he felt the plane's engines shut off. Beside him Cassie whimpered, keen to leave the vehicle.

Before accepting the job at Fossil Bluff, Will insisted that Cassie be able to accompany him. He had no doubt that she would enjoy the adventure and, as she was a Siberian Husky, Will felt that she would easily acclimatise to the low temperatures. The British Antarctic Survey had no issues with Cassie joining the team, even allowing her to sit in the passenger area of the private plane, rather than in the cargo hold. As Will and Cassie were the only passengers, there had been no one to complain anyway. He could only hope that the rest of the team, whom he was yet to meet, would be welcoming of her.

The exit door opened with a hiss of hydraulics as the steward announced it was time to leave the aircraft. Will struggled with his hand luggage as Cassie pulled on her leash, desperate to find fresh air and relieve herself.

"We'll bring your luggage through shortly," the steward stated as Will was almost dragged down the steps by Cassie. "Head up to the red building," he said with a nod. Will reached the bottom of the steps and Cassie immediately squatted, turning the snow yellow beneath her.

"Feel better?" he asked. Cassie was whimpering again, seemingly confused by the cold, white powder on her paws. "I know," Will comforted. "You'll get used to it." The red building, known as 'The Hut', was less than twenty metres away, and the pair trudged through the snow as quickly as they could manage. *Perhaps this is going to be harder than I had expected?* Will wondered. He had worked as a researcher for the British Antarctic Survey for almost ten years but had never had the opportunity to visit the place. Most research trips took place in the summer months and there were a huge number of experts desperate for the chance to go. This would be the first winter stay that anyone had volunteered for in over twenty years and would be one of the longest at almost seven months.

*Seven months of almost continuous darkness. Seven months with no way home,* Will mused as he pushed the door to The Hut open. The warmth hit him first, followed closely by the smell of food cooking. He kept hold of Cassie's leash until he had introduced himself to the other members of the team, more for the safety of anyone's meal than anything else. The Hut could accommodate up to six people, and these spaces were easily filled during the summer expeditions. The work this team carried out only required three people and The Hut felt all the more spacious for it. Inside was a small living space consisting of three small sofas and a coffee table. There was a dining table which could only seat four at a time, an open-plan cooking area, and three sets of bunk beds.

"Hi," Will said, closing the door behind

him. "I'm Will, and this is Cassie." At the stove, stirring saucepan of tinned soup, stood a woman around Will's age. She was as tall as him, thin, with brown hair tied in a bun.

"I'm Heather," she replied with a smile. "That's Gunther over there." Will looked towards one of the bunks where a man in his fifties was staring at a laptop with his earphones in. He glanced up at the new arrivals and gave a nod before continuing with whatever he was watching. "Are you hungry?" Heather asked.

"Yeah, a bit. Thanks. Are you okay with the dog if I let her off?"

"Of course," Heather said, approaching Cassie to give her head a stroke. "It'll be nice having an animal around that isn't another penguin!" Will watched as Heather poured the soup into three mugs, taking the first over to Gunther. Cassie jumped as the door behind them swung open, the pilot and steward making their way in, dragging Will's cases behind them. Will thanked them and took his belongings over to the vacant bunk while the aircraft crew chatted with Heather and enjoyed a hot drink before flying off again.

Gunther barely moved from his laptop the rest of that day and so it fell to Heather to show Will around. Will learned that his two teammates had arrived a week prior to him and had been tasked with taking inventory and ensuring everything was in order before he arrived. Will was shown to the toilet and shower room which was part of the adjacent building, alongside the food and water stores. Food either came in tins or was already freeze-dried and could be prepared by adding hot water.

"The biggest downside is having the toilet in a separate building," Heather commented. "More so because if you wake up in the night needing to go, you have to get all the kit on first. You really wouldn't want to come out here in just a dressing gown!" Will simply nodded, gazing out of the window at the vast expanse of ice and snow.

The tour was brief, as there really wasn't much to see, and the trio (plus Cassie) spent Will's first evening going over the agenda for the coming months. There was little to do besides work but, at that point, Will felt that he could easily cope with the situation. After all, it had been his dream to visit Antarctica.

*Day Twenty-four*

Less than a month into the winter stay-over, Will had settled in as well as could be expected. He had thrown himself into his work (the collection and study of the very limited plant life, which mostly consisted of lichens and algae) and even Cassie seemed to be content lazing about in The Hut and helping to carry some of the equipment on the short expeditions to the coast.

The days had become almost non-existent, providing a window of only a few hours in which to safely travel. A routine fixed itself in place, so much so that Will began to lose track of the days. Each morning would begin with him pulling on his snowsuit and trudging over to the shower room. The trio alternated who would prepare breakfast, which almost always consisted of porridge or baked beans, and then they would discuss their plans for the day. The British Antarctic Survey had been kind enough to ship enough dog food to Fossil Bluff so that Cassie's presence wouldn't cause any problems with the rationing, but the cost of the food had come out of Will's wages.

Day twenty-four began no differently to the previous ones; Will showered, walked Cassie around the buildings a few times, and sat down to the porridge which Gunther had prepared. Will informed the others that he was to head back to the coast to gather samples, expecting to be out for no more than two hours. It was a given that he would take Cassie with him.

"Do you mind if I join you?" Heather asked. This caught Will off-guard, having only ventured out with his dog, and Heather immediately noticed the hesitation in his voice. "I've caught up on most of my work and I'm going a little stir-crazy here all day. I could do with a walk."

"Of course," Will replied. "It'd be nice to have some company." Cassie whimpered. "I meant human company," Will told her. Once breakfast was over Will packed a bag with the necessary equipment and attached Cassie's leash. "Ready?" he called over to Heather.

Heather gave him a light-hearted salute before calling over to Gunther. "See you in a couple of hours."

"Uh-huh," was all he could manage, not bothering to look up from his laptop.

*** 

The sun had only risen a little, despite it being late morning, and Will knew that it would not rise much higher. This would be the tenth time he had taken this journey and barely needed the compass at all,

128

even though the landscape appeared the same in each direction. The walk to the coast would have taken only fifteen minutes anywhere else in the world, but on the treacherous ice plains it took more than twice that. Will had given himself an hour at the site in which to gather samples, a job which ended up taking less time with Heather's help.

"It's beautiful out here," Heather remarked, watching a group of seals soak up the last of the day's sunshine.

"Yes," Will agreed. "But I'm wondering if seven months may be too long?"

"Perhaps, but there is no way back until the summer starts. They won't fly us off until the weather is good enough. It's a good job if the cold is the worst thing we have to contend with. I've heard some horror stories about polar bear attacks in the Arctic."

"Can't blame them really," Will pointed out. "Global warming equals less food for the bears. They're starving and therefore more dangerous."

"Absolutely. I just mean I'm glad we don't have that threat hanging over us."

"I wouldn't worry anyway; Cassie will keep us safe." The Husky looked up at her owner and gave out a small bark, almost as though she had understood the

129

conversation.

***

Will found that having company on the trip had caused the time to fly by, and he was surprised to see that the intended hour had turned into almost two. The collection of samples may have happened quicker with two pairs of hands, but more time had passed in conversation. Fearing that it would get dark before they made it back, Will, Heather, and Cassie packed up the equipment and started their hike to The Hut. Ten minutes into the journey Cassie bounded ahead. The two humans surveyed the ground ahead of them in search of something other than the brilliant white and their gaze landed on a dark lump just as Cassie reached it. Will sped up, calling out his dog's name, fearing that she was going to try to eat whatever it was. Cassie backed off, watching her master and waiting for further instructions. It took Will a few moments to process what lay before him. Heather spoke first.

"That's impossible," she declared, looking from the carcass on the snow to Will and back again. In front of them were the remains of a seal; head still intact but entrails spread across the snow. The wound to its body was deep, flesh torn away in chunks as though the damage had been caused by a ferocious set of teeth.

"What could have done that?" Will asked, his voice taking on a small shake. "The only predators to seals around here are killer whales, but we're too far inland." Heather tried to come up with a sensible suggestion, but she had nothing to offer. Attacks on seals only happened in the sea, that was a fact. The only other land creatures for hundreds of miles were penguins and there was no way they could have caused this damage.

"We should get back to The Hut," Heather stated, her pace quickening. Will followed, before realising that Cassie had not moved from her spot by the dead seal.

"Cassie! Come on, girl!" Will yelled. The hair on Cassie's back was raised and even through his hat and hood Will could hear her soft growl. He scoped the horizon but could see nothing out of the ordinary. Something had gotten Cassie worked up and Will trusted the dog's instincts more than his own. Reattaching her leash, Will tugged at the Husky and the pair almost ran to catch up with Heather.

Gunther seemed far less concerned

131

about the dead seal than Will and Heather had been, despite agreeing that it was out of the ordinary. It had clearly been attacked by something larger than itself, something which should not be found in that area, but with nothing else to go on there was little that could be done and work quickly resumed.

*Day Thirty-nine*

Will had been reluctant to take the same trip since the discovery of the seal carcass but he knew it was unavoidable. He was thankful that he had enough samples to work on for at least two weeks but the time to venture beyond the perceived safety of The Hut soon came around.

"Is anyone free to come with me?" Will asked after the team had finished their breakfasts.

"Still scared of the mysterious seal killer?" Gunther teased.

"I wouldn't say scared," Will replied. "Wary may be a better word."

"I've got too much to do here," Heather said. "I got a bit behind and the weekly report is due soon. Go with him Gunther; it won't take long." Gunther managed a grunt but suited-up for the trek anyway.

Visibility was far worse than on

previous excursions; the high winds blowing the powdery snow about in front of their faces so they could see only a few metres ahead of themselves. Will decided to keep Cassie on her leash, fearful they would lose her in the snowstorm. Barely ten minutes into the walk the dog stopped dead, feet firmly planted into the icy ground, tail down, fur up. Something spooked her, even more so than before, and the growl she emitted was like nothing Will had ever heard from her before.

Gunther and Will looked at one another, both unsettled, neither willing to take another step forward until Cassie gave the all clear. They looked ahead, attempting to make out any shapes that may not belong on this frozen continent, but could see nothing.

"What do you think?" Will shouted above the howl of the wind and the guttural growl of his dog.

"She doesn't look like she wants to go on," Gunther shouted in reply. "Maybe we should head back?" Through the protective goggles Will could see fear on the older man's face - fear of something unknown yet undeniably present. "We can try again when the weather improves. I don't like not being able to see what's ahead of us," Gunther continued. Will

133

nodded, tugging at the leash.

"Come on Cassie, let's go." The dog seemed to understand the command and turned quickly, as though relieved to be returning to The Hut. Cassie bounded all the way back, almost dragging Will. The trio moved as quickly as possible, never stopping to look back.

Hearing the account from Gunther set Heather into panic mode. He was always the sensible one, dismissive of anything he couldn't see for himself, seemingly afraid of nothing. Even though nobody had actually *seen* anything, the two men were clearly shaken.

"We should contact H.Q.," Heather said. "I'm almost finished with my report. I told them about the seal we found but they gave no reply, so I presume they didn't find it concerning."

"If they weren't interested in the seal then I don't see them being bothered about the dog acting crazy," Gunther replied. "But you may as well mention it in the report. Just in case."

"In case what?" Will asked, his eyes betraying the fear he still felt.

"I don't know," Gunther continued. "Maybe we'll find another seal, or a penguin. We have some night-vision cameras left from the summer team who were filming penguins. We need some way to see what's going on out there without putting ourselves in direct danger."

"You think we're in danger?" Heather asked. Saying the words aloud somehow added weight to them.

"I'm not sure," Gunther answered honestly. "Perhaps it's nothing."

"Either way," Will said, "it wouldn't hurt to have the cameras working. If we work together it won't take long."

The team set to work rigging up four cameras, one around ten metres from each corner of The Hut. The footage fed through to Gunther's laptop, the green haze of the night-vision showing nothing aside from the swirling of snow. Gunther tapped a button and a howling sound came through the laptop's tiny speakers, nothing more than the wind, so he turned off the sound.

"Now what?" Will asked. "We just watch the screen and look out for monsters?"

"It's probably nothing," Gunther said with a shrug. "Probably."

*Day Forty-six*

The first six nights of camera footage showed nothing out of the ordinary. However, it was the footage of the seventh night that was enough to give the team nightmares. Gunther half-heartedly sat through the previous night's footage, sped up to thirty-two times the recording rate, enabling him to view the nine hours of video in less than twenty minutes. Heather and Will made more coffee while the footage played, wanting to know that it was all clear before trying to concentrate on the day's work. Heather nearly spilled the coffee she was pouring as Gunther jumped, almost sending the metal chair crashing to the ground.

"Fuck me," Gunther said, eyes still transfixed on the screen. Will and Heather looked at one another.

"What is it?" Heather asked as they made their way around to Gunther. The screen showed another dead seal, sporting similar injuries to the one found three weeks prior.

"You need to see this," Gunther replied, his shaking hands working the laptop to rewind the footage. He dragged the cursor back by less than a minute and played it in real time. The hazy green screen showed a clear night; white snow covered the ground and stars could be made out in the sky. Then they saw it, appearing without warning in front of the camera to the south. The team couldn't have asked for a clearer image, although this was not a sight any of them wished to see.

With hoofed feet, the creature stood upright on two legs. Humanoid in shape, but not in features, the monster was the size of a tall man. Its entire body was covered in lightly coloured fur, muscular, elongated arms holding the bleeding corpse of the seal up to its face as it fed. Even through the night vision lens, dark spots on its chest were visible which Gunther suggested was most likely blood. It wasn't until the creature discarded the meal that the team could see its face.

A dark spattering of seal blood covered its mouth and chin. The face was reminiscent of a ram's, with an elongated snout and small ears which lie tucked away behind menacing spiralled horns. It was a creature of myth and legend, an abomination to all that is good, and a potential danger to the three humans so far from home. Once it had abandoned the seal's carcass to the ice the creature quickly turned its head, staring right into the camera as though it knew what it was.

"Yeti?" Heather asked, barely believing the words as they left her mouth. Will and Gunther looked at her, not to mock but with consideration. Gunther slammed the laptop shut.

"What do we do?" Will asked. "We have to tell someone and get out of here!" He was unable to hide the panic rising in his voice. The Hut started to feel too small around him.

"Okay," Gunther began. "We all saw that, right? So, there's no denying there is something out there." Everyone nodded as Gunther sat processing the events with scientific logic. "I can isolate that part of the footage once I've viewed the rest; that way we can send it over to London and request an evacuation. However..." Gunther paused.

"However what Gunther?" Will asked. "They have to come get us!"

"And I'm sure they will try, but it'll depend on weather conditions." Gunther paused, reluctant to voice his concerns. "They may also want us to study it," he said quietly.

"Shit," Heather muttered. "You're right but that's not what we're here for. I never signed up for that!"

"Fuck that," Will replied. "If they want to catch that thing then they need to send in the sort of people that do that. Military, or whatever. We don't have any weapons and I'm not going back out there until a plane arrives."

"And what about when you need a

piss?" Gunther asked. He had a good point and Will knew it.

"We go in pairs," Heather suggested. "And take the dog. She was good at sensing when that thing was nearby." They agreed and set to work on contacting London to explain the situation. Gunther sorted out the right piece of footage, Heather wrote down exactly what had happened and what they expected HQ to do about it, and Will stared intently at the live footage which was streaming through one of the monitors at the work station, oblivious to his coffee which was cooling in his hands.

The team caught no sight of the creature the rest of that day while taking trips to the storeroom/shower room in pairs and with Cassie by their side. Adrenalin pumped all day and by evening everything felt so distant that they started wondering if what they had seen was even real.

"We should all get some sleep, there should be some news tomorrow," Gunther announced after checking comms for a reply from London for the tenth time. Will double-checked the doors and windows, going so far as to push one of the sofas in front of the main entrance. Nobody slept well that night, tossing and turning in the bunks, listening for the sound of anything out of the ordinary.

*Day Forty-seven*

Will awoke to Cassie growling in the darkness. He could hear the others stirring and called his dog, whispering her name.

"Cassie," he called out, quietly. "What is it?" A light flicked on beside Heather's bed as she sat up. Her gaze flicked from Will to Cassie. The Husky had climbed on to the sofa against the door so that her head was level with the doorknob. Cassie's fur was on end just as before, and her growl seemed to continue in one long breath. Something was outside, of that there was no doubt.

A crash against the front door sent Cassie yelping in fear as she leapt from the sofa and took position a few feet further back. Once in place she resumed the warning growl, not moving from the spot as the three humans got to their feet and stood behind the dog.

Another crash against the wooden door and everybody jumped. Whatever was out there wanted in. Gunther suddenly sprang to his bunk and dragged a bag out from underneath. He pulled two flare guns from

140

the bag, tossing one to Will.

"It'll have to do," he announced with a shrug, before switching on the monitor to display the live feed from outside. The cameras faced away from The Hut so they showed nothing of the main entrance.

"If we stay quiet it might go away," Heather said, trying to hold back tears.

"It was quiet in here when it arrived," Will pointed out. "It might be able to smell us, or..." He was interrupted by another crash at the door, this time accompanied by the sound of wood splitting.

"The door won't hold!" Gunther yelled, loading the flare gun and pointing it at the entry point. There came another crash, followed by yet another. The creature seemed aware of their presence now and was determined to get inside. The group held their position.

One final attack against the door and it gave, coming away at the hinges. Frozen in panic, Will watched as two clawed hands lifted the detached door from its position against the sofa and hurled it out of the way. Cassie's growl turned to an angry bark; there was nowhere for the flight reflex to take her, so fight was the only option.

For a split-second the creature simply stood, arms by its side, almost surprised by the people it saw inside. It was taller than they had expected, having to bend down to fit through the door frame. Gunther was the first to fire, the flare hissing forward and passing the creature's head by no more than an inch. An unearthly howl came from it as it acknowledged the attack and it leapt over the sofa and straight for Gunther.

Will had no time to fire his flare before the creature's razor-sharp claws were at Gunther's throat. Will took a few steps back as he stared in horror at the sight; thick spurts of crimson spraying from the wound in Gunther's neck, his eyes staring at his killer with confusion.

"Shoot it!" Heather screamed, backing herself against the wall. Will registered what she said and raised the flare gun. The creature turned to face Will, tilting its head forward slightly as though threatening him with the deadly horns on its head.

It charged. Will pulled the trigger. The gun jammed.

Will was certain he was about to die so when the creature fell backwards it took him by surprise. The room filled with the most horrific sounds as Cassie's growls mingled with those of the creature. Will's faithful Husky had launched herself at this monstrosity, teeth deeply embedded into its right thigh.

Will couldn't look away as the creature swiped at Cassie, its claws struggling to find their target yet only taking off chunks of fur. Even so, Will knew it wouldn't be long before that thing landed a successful blow. It would only take one hit from those deadly talons in the right place to finish Cassie. Will raised the flare gun once more and the creature looked at him, seeming to know what was coming. For a split-second Will was sure he could see fear in the monster's eyes.

He pulled the trigger.

The flare whooshed towards its target and landed exactly where it was meant to, albeit with disappointing results. The flare hit the creature square in the face but there was no explosion of flames. It was, however, enough to disorientate the monster, sending it scrambling backwards. Cassie released the fleshy thigh as the beast fell back. Before it could move to attack again, the dog was at the pale fur around the creature's throat, teeth embedded firmly. Will watched as their attacker tried to find the strength to lift its long arms, to no avail. Finally, when the creature had twitched for the last time, Cassie let go and ran to be beside her owner.

*Day Fifty*

Favourable weather conditions allowed for Will, Heather, and Cassie to be evacuated within days of their encounter. Gunther had been correct about the British Antarctic Survey wanting to study the thing that had attacked them. Will resented the excitement his superiors showed when he told them they had the body, or at least most of it.

The plane arrived with more crew and equipment than before. The body of the monster was wrapped and loaded into the hold, whereas Gunther's body was prepared and laid, as respectfully as possible, in the gangway between seats. Heather, Will, and no doubt Cassie, were relieved to take their seats on the plane and watched the red building grow smaller as they began their ascent.

"Back to civilisation," Heather said with a sigh. Will said nothing, watching as two tall, horned creatures approached The Hut.

# The Devil's Triangle

Being a bit of a loner, the job suited me well. So well, in fact, that I rarely took my allocated weeks of leave. I was contracted for three weeks on, followed by one week off, but due to low staff numbers the powers that be were happy for me to stay aboard. I could never understand why they found it difficult to recruit cooks for the cargo shipping industry – the pay is decent, the job is easy enough for anyone with kitchen experience, and you get a roof over your head. Perhaps 'normal' people don't like to be away from everyone for weeks at a time. And perhaps I'd feel the same if I actually had anyone to spend time with.

With the crew alternating quite regularly, I met a lot of people but nobody I'd call a friend. Seven years in the job and I only knew a handful of names. The crew may have changed with most voyages, but this ship was my home – The Atlantis. Regardless of who was working alongside me, one thing had become evident from the very beginning – sailors are a superstitious bunch. I almost got a hiding when I first started due to my whistling in the kitchen. I thought it had just been irritating for the other men, but they genuinely believed it would 'whistle up a storm'! And I can't even tell you how many pig and rooster tattoos I've seen. It was due to this level of superstition that, I believe, left us especially short-staffed that day.

A new route had been added to our roster, sailing from El Puerto de Santa Maria in Spain to Havana, Cuba, and then on to Lisbon in Portugal. I'd never been to Cuba and was quite excited about the two-night stopover in Havana which would break up the month-long round trip. What had set the crew on edge, I quickly learned, was having to pass through the Bermuda Triangle. I laughed (inwardly, of course) at what seemed to be an irrational fear of something as believable as Bigfoot or the Loch Ness Monster. Superstitions are one thing, but these men were genuinely nervous about the journey. I, on the other hand, kept my mind on Havana, women, and rum.

Clear skies and a flat ocean made for steady progress for a full ten days. The atmosphere onboard was tense, however, seeming to get more so as we approached our destination. I worked longer days than usual, preparing three meals a day, and clearing up afterwards. I'd flop into my bunk late each evening when my work was finally done, knowing I needed to be back in the kitchen first thing the next morning. Those ten days flew by. On the eleventh day, we entered The Devil's Triangle.

It was as though God himself had flicked a switch. The clear skies and still waters we had been graced with changed in a moment as we crossed the mythical boundary. The sunlight which had been streaming through the windows to the kitchen suddenly disappeared, only to be replaced with the dull grey darkness of heavy cloud cover, forcing me to turn on the lights. Shouts could be heard from the corridor as panic began to take hold and I must admit that even I felt a wave of nervousness wash over me. *Just a storm,* I told myself, *we've been through plenty of those.*

Not wanting to get involved with the nonsense the crew were saying, I kept my head down and continued preparing the lunches. Heavy-booted feet ran past but the kitchen door remained closed – even if

147

there was any danger, nobody came to check on me. This went on for around thirty minutes as I continued working, ignoring the rocking of the ship as best I could. Rain hammered against the windows, pots and pans slid across stainless-steel work surfaces, and then the lights went out.

The kitchen was plunged into darkness and the rocking of the ship intensified. I grabbed hold of a worktop to steady myself, allowing my eyes to adjust. A crack of lightning lit up the room for a fraction of a second, immediately followed by the loudest rumble of thunder I had ever heard. I knew we were in for a bumpy ride, yet still I paid no mind to the tales of The Devil's Triangle, convincing myself that it was just another storm, albeit a pretty severe one. Until the sirens started.

I knew by this point that I needed more information, that hiding out in the kitchen was not my best course of action. The sirens that had joined the hellish thunder were inducing a sense of panic and the darkness didn't help either. I had only ever heard those sirens during training exercises and I knew what this particular tone implied – we were at risk of hitting something. Although, there shouldn't be anything *to* hit.

Pulling open the heavy metal door, I found the corridor deserted. The phrase *'All hands on deck'* sprang to mind and I made my way towards the bridge. This journey involved ascending one flight of steps and a quick trip across the deck, something I wasn't happy about doing during a storm. I reached the top of the steps and found the door. Outside was thick with darkness, despite being late morning. The rain continued to lash against the door, and I looked for the other crew but could see no-one.

For the first time in my life, I felt a rush of nausea as the ship rolled side to side and I could just make out the horizon as it appeared to tip to a terrifying degree. Seeing the deck as empty as the corridors didn't sit right and my eyes wandered up to the bridge. I could make out the illumination from the various control panels but there were no figures moving around in there. *Where had they all gone?* Assuming they were hunkered down somewhere, I chose not to venture outside. Instead, I made my way back down the stairs, towards the sleeping quarters. It was the only place left to check and I could feel an anger rising within me. If I found everyone huddled together, nobody having bothered to check on me, then I'd lose my temper with them.

My walk towards the cabins became a march as I convinced myself that was where I would find them. The sight of the deserted cabins was the final straw and I allowed myself to sink to the floor. They had to be onboard, but where? I was about to continue my search when a nerve-shredding screech of metal outweighed even the thunder and the sirens. At first, I thought the huge shipping containers had begun sliding across the deck, but I quickly realised the horrific truth. We *had* hit something, something large enough to tear a hole in the bow. The sound of metal on metal continued for painful seconds, as though some giant, metallic sea monster were ripping our vessel apart. I felt the ship lurch to one side before the screeching stopped, only to replaced by an even worse sound – the splashing of water.

We were going down, of this I had no doubt, and my training suddenly kicked in. I knew what I needed to do, but actually doing it was a different matter. The ship continued to turn to one side, and I knew it wouldn't be long before it began to disappear beneath the surface. My ascent to deck level was made more difficult by the awkward angle but I made it, thrusting open the door. The two lifeboats located on the starboard side were now dangling precariously in the air as that side of the ship rose higher. Port side was my best bet, I decided, certain I could slide down the deck and detach a lifeboat which was almost at sea level anyway.

I was under no illusions that I'd fair any better in a lifeboat, but it was that or let the ship drag me down with it, so I eased myself out the door. Laying on the slippery deck, I clung to the doorframe, feet hanging towards the submerged port side. The railings at the edge of the deck were only a few feet above the surging water as I let go of the door and allowed myself to drop onto them. Thankfully, I didn't disappear through any of the gaps, managing to sit on the railings and edge my way along to the nearest lifeboat. Climbing inside, I took one last look across The Atlantis for any sign of life and, satisfied there was nothing more I could do, I released the chains.

I positioned myself across the bottom of the lifeboat, eyes closed, blocking out the stomach-turning rise and fall of the waves. The small craft stayed afloat for longer than The Atlantis but not by much. I felt a heavy crash of water hitting my back, followed by a smack to the head as I collided with the side of the lifeboat. I felt my body slide off the hard surface and an even thicker darkness surround me. My legs kicked against water as my mind processed what had happened – the lifeboat had capsized, and I was hidden underneath it. Designed to carry more than twenty people, the lifeboat was far too large for me to flip over. I took a breath and lunged deeper, swimming beneath the edge of the boat with the intention of climbing onto its underside. I quickly learned that this was futile; I was weakened from the events and could not find purchase on the wet surface. Hopelessness enveloped me and, at that moment, I gave up. I took in one final gasp of air and allowed the sea to swallow me, blackness soon filling my mind.

I woke up, briefly convinced it must have been some horrendous nightmare. As I took in my surroundings, all I felt was confusion. I had awoken on the ground within some kind of cave, soft piles of kelp beneath me. Out of reflex, I reached to my head to inspect the wound I had received as the lifeboat capsized, only to find it had been bandaged. My clothes were inexplicably dry, and I felt as though I had slept well. *If I've been rescued, then why am I not in a hospital?* I pondered, surveying my surroundings. The cavern I found myself in was well-lit by brilliant white orbs which had been placed a few feet apart, just above head height. I could see no obvious power supply, but I was certain they weren't natural.

Dragging myself to my feet, I took slow steps around the cave, examining the lights and looking for any signs of life. I called out a *hello*, but my voice sounded unpleasantly loud as it bounced off the hard walls. Having received no reply, I stood in the centre of the cave, perplexed. There was no obvious way in or out, but logic said that one must exist. Someone

153

had taken care of me, had placed me here to rest, and had left. As my mind wandered, trying to assess my situation with such little information, my thoughts were interrupted by a whooshing sound from behind me. The sudden noise startled me, and I turned, jaw opening in shock as a doorway appeared in the cave wall. It reminded me of old science fiction shows on television, the rock seeming to glide open, revealing a tunnel illuminated with the same glowing orbs. Still, there was no sign of life.

Knowing I had no choice, I hesitantly stepped into the corridor, the door again causing me to start as it closed behind me. I took around twenty cautious steps along the corridor before it split into two, with no suggestion as to which route to take. Arbitrarily choosing to head to the right, I wondered what had caused the door to open when it did. Was I being watched? Had I done something to make it open? More importantly, who, or what, had rescued me?

The tunnels led into a wider opening and an odd sensation came over me. My first impression was that it reminded me of an aquarium – the large, convex glass revealing the depths of the ocean beyond. That impressive sight gave way to the feeling of absolute horror as I now knew I was still deep within the sea with no obvious way to return to the surface. I approached the glass, which must have been at least thirty feet high, and looked out at the ocean floor. What should have been a pit of darkness was brightly lit by glowing orbs, lights which appeared to simply float in place, and which illuminated a heap of sunken vessels for as far as I could see. There were yachts and ships, even a cruise liner and a navy transporter, as well as planes of varying sizes. Rusted metal blades protruded from the wreckage which may well have once been the propellers of a helicopter. My gaze of both wonderment and fear was interrupted by an agonizing scream.

A door flung open at one side of the room as a man ran towards me. I did not recognise him as one of The Atlantis' crew and he was shouting something in a language I couldn't understand, Russian, perhaps? He held one hand to the opposite arm as he ran, blood dripping from the wound he was trying to contain. I froze, unsure whether to run or to help, and he

155

was less than six feet away from me when he dropped to the floor. At first, he appeared to have tripped over his own feet but then I saw it – the grip of one thick, purplish tentacle was wrapped around his right ankle. Before I could reach out to him, he was yanked back and dragged through the door.

In an act of uncharacteristic bravery, I followed. Whatever was going on, I needed to know. My mind raced with all the old myths about The Devil's Triangle - tales of aliens, sea monsters, government conspiracies. Whatever that thing was, it had nothing to do with the government. This structure and the medical care I'd received ruled out sea monsters. Seeing what I could see, the final option didn't sound so ridiculous.

The thin trail of blood led me in the right direction and I soon found myself on what could loosely be described as a hospital ward. I passed several rooms, most housing a patient, each one confined to their bed. I wondered why I had awoken in that cave, rather than here. The blood trail led me to a room in which the man was now strapped to a bed, various machines attached to him as he shook

156

violently. There was no sign of the owner of the tentacle and so I moved on, finding myself at another door.

With no keypad, no handle, and no obvious lock, I hammered on the door looking for answers. None came. I moved from room to room, unable to gain entry to any of them. Some patients appeared to be sleeping, or even comatose, while others thrashed against their binds. Whatever fiend had returned that man to his room was behind that final door, of that I was certain, so I returned with determination. I attacked the door with all my strength, hitting it until my hands had turned red. Eventually, the racket I was making must have been enough as the door slid open revealing a sight that caused my bladder to release.

Humanoid in shape, three creatures stood before me. Their green, reptilian faces made me think back to old episodes of Doctor Who. A little taller than the average man, they appeared almost scaly. The word amphibious came to mind. They had arms not dissimilar to human arms, but with webbing between the four fingers, yet they had a nest of legs formed of thick, muscular tentacles. Beyond them in that room were rows of specimen jars and screens displaying symbols I had never seen before. Slowly, I took a step backwards, then I turned to run.

I met the same fate as my Russian friend, feeling something wrap around my ankle before my face hit the cold floor. My nose cracked, blood pooling around my face. I expected to suddenly be dragged away but my assailants were coming to me, instead. I stood no chance against three of them, or one of them, quite possibly, and I found myself being carried to an unused room.

They were too strong for me to fight against, two creatures pinning me to the bed as the other fixed the restraints in place. I tried to talk to them, to plead, to understand what was happening but I was ignored. It quickly became obvious that I was just another specimen, an animal to them. I could only assume that I had been cared for and allowed to rest so that I'd be in peak condition.

I don't know how long ago that was. I tried to keep track of the days but without any discernible night and day, I soon lost count. I know it's been weeks, possibly months. I wondered many times what would have happened if I'd taken a different route out of that cave, if I hadn't hammered on that door, if I'd tried to run. But those kind of thoughts can drive a person insane. The fact is that I'm now here, in this experimental horror show, undoubtedly for the rest of my life. I'm not the same person I was, not just because of the terrors I witnessed, but physically I'm changing. I don't know what has been done to me here because I'm unconscious most of the time, but I know some 'procedures' have taken place. I haven't seen my body below the shoulders for some time, unable to move the heavy sheet placed over me. My little fingers seem to be shrinking and a thin layer of skin appears to be forming between the other four. Deep down I know what is happening, but my mind won't allow me to recognise it. It blocks out the unmistakable green tint to my skin, the ache in my jaw as my face takes on its new shape, the odd sensation of my legs beneath the sheet. I am being reborn.

# The Place Between Worlds

There was no real build-up to *that* night. Nothing comes to mind as having been out of the ordinary. That said, it was not entirely out of the blue either. It was as if I knew something was going to happen, something terrifying, but I could do nothing to prevent it. After all, sleep will take you eventually, no matter how hard you try to fight it. Two nights previously I had a dream. This wasn't unusual for me of late. I had given up alcohol in an attempt to become healthier and save a few pennies, so I had not been falling straight into a deep, dreamless sleep. My mind had been racing each evening, thinking over my plans for the next day, fantasizing about the murders of colleagues who had pissed me off, wondering if I would ever have the courage to date again. This last thought was always the most prevalent, as fears of eternal loneliness led to thoughts of Emily and the fact she was gone. Not dead, but she may as well have been. She'd walked out after a fight, one in which I was drunk again, and never came back. She had ghosted me ever since.

This life-shattering event caused me to drink even more than I already was, wallowing in self-pity, barely clinging onto my job. I was a mess, genuinely not caring what happened to me, until one day something clicked. Yes, I was heartbroken, but this was no way to continue. So, I kicked the booze and did all those things that people say help - I started eating properly, exercising, and keeping the flat clean. I shouldn't have been surprised, but it really did help. After two months without Emily, I could finally see a change in my life. That didn't stop me dreaming about her though.

As I mentioned earlier, two nights previous to *that* night, I had a dream. It was more like half a dream, if that makes sense, but I guess no dreams really reach a logical conclusion. Emily was there, standing at the edge of a foreboding forest, wearing a red cape and hood, wicker basket in hand as if she belonged in a fairy-tale. I could feel myself approaching her, certain that she was looking at me. There was a sadness in her eyes, and she could not even manage a smile for me but, somehow, I felt that we were going to embrace, perhaps even work things out. I got to within a few feet of her and the sky erupted with a flash of lightning, causing Emily to look to the heavens with panic on her face. Before I could get any closer, she turned on her heels and ran. At this point I woke up.

I hadn't thought much of it during the next day, putting it down to the fact that I missed Emily so deeply. The dream had been eerie, the woods at night having always heightened my anxiety, but the premise of Emily running from me was sadly self-explanatory. I had spent the day at work as usual, keeping to myself, and then had spent two hours at the gym. The exercise really did help, and I was in a good mood by the time I returned to my bed.

I had never experienced recurring dreams before, but this was stranger still. In my dream state, I found myself approaching the entrance to the same forest, Emily exactly as she had been on the previous night. This time, however, there was a familiarity about the scene. It was as though, despite it being a dream, I could remember being there before. I continued on my path towards Emily,

162

looking up to the sky a moment *before* the lightning illuminated the dense clouds. I knew what would happen, I heard myself call out her name, but she still turned and ran.

My first thought was that I would awaken at that point, so I must have known that I was in a dream. A rumble of thunder brought me back to myself as the heavens opened, and a gale blew rain into my face. It's hard to explain whether it was a conscious decision, or simply the obvious thing to do, but I ran into the forest. I couldn't say if it was merely for shelter from the storm, or to follow Emily. Quite likely it was both. The darkness was virtually impenetrable only ten feet into the woods, the only break from the darkness coming as the lightning cracked overhead giving a split-second view of what lay before me. Nothing but blackened, gnarled branches surrounded me, and I got just the briefest glimpse of a red hood in the distance before she was gone completely.

I woke this time trembling, my bedsheets dampened by sweat. This had been more unsettling than the previous night's dream, the feeling of dread

163

permeating through to my waking hours. Yet, despite the pain of seeing Emily run from me, regardless of the terror I felt in those dark and threatening woods, I longed to go back. Somehow, I knew that I had no choice, and I spent the whole day in anticipation of bedtime.

It was ironic really that I was so nervous and excited about getting back to the dream, I found it much harder to fall asleep. I thought about picking up a book but feared that the story would influence what I dreamed about. The same argument was made for not watching a film, so I settled for some comedy show that was on yet another rerun. I became afraid that I would get no further into the dream, as the time I had left for sleep was growing shorter, so I switched off my alarm. I'd call in sick if I didn't wake up in time naturally. I then pondered how time appears in dreams, how it isn't linear at all, how dreams can span days or weeks, and it was as I thought about this that I must have drifted off. And *that* was the night that changed everything.

It's dark, and I'm approaching the entrance to a forest. When I say entrance, it's really just a small gap but the path I am on seems to lead there. The tree line stretches as far as I can see to my left and right, with no other obvious entry points. As before, Emily stands at the entrance, dressed in red, looking at me. At least I think she is looking at me; she shows no expression on her face. The now-expected flash of lightning comes, I call out her name, and she runs. I pick up my pace, hoping to reach the shelter of the trees before the heavens open, and almost make it. The thunder roars, the wind blows; it is as it was before. Almost.

Dead branches crack under my feet as I fumbled my way into the forest. The darkness was as thick as I remembered it but there was something else, a nagging thought. *You remembered!* I told myself, reaching into my pocket and retrieving the thin torch. I twisted it on, pointing the beam at the uneven floor beneath me. I knew I was in a dream, but it seemed partially under my control. This was possibly the strangest feeling I have ever had. I shone the light as far ahead as I could and caught another glimpse of Emily's red hood disappearing around a large tree. I called out to her once again, but she could not have heard me over the sound of the thunder and the wind shaking the trees. I needed to catch up with her.

Traversing the forest was difficult, with branches and detritus littering the narrow path. Considering how hard I was finding it, I could not fathom how Emily was able to move so quickly without a light to guide her. My own torch was concentrated on the ground immediately in front of me most of the time, but occasionally I would raise it in search of Emily. I spotted her in the distance on a number of occasions, always slightly too far away. Time is impossible to measure in a dream, but I was exhausted from the hike through the forest. I felt as though I had been walking for hours, with no end in sight.

The direction that I was taking seemed intuitive, but I'd had enough. *Perhaps this was the lesson I needed to learn?* I pondered. *No matter how long I chase her for, she won't come back. Maybe I just need to give up.* I turned around with every intention of heading back the way I had come, only to find the path I had taken was now inaccessible. The trees appeared to have spread their finger-like branches out to one another, removing any chance of me finding a way through. My journey was out of my hands, if it had ever actually been under my control. The forest wanted me to go on; this place had an unnerving hold over me and all I could do was obey.

I slept in my dream, as bizarre as that sounds. I must have walked for days, and on two occasions I could see myself, from outside of my body, sleeping in the dirt. I can only assume that day and night passed in that place, but the darkness of the forest remained constant. I never felt hungry or thirsty, never needed the bathroom, but the exhaustion from the hike was unmistakable. I remember thinking how pleased I was that I'd been exercising regularly, and then told myself not to be stupid as I'd only been doing that in the 'real world'. Everything became confusing by this point, and I never expected to leave that place.

What I believe represented my fourth day in the forest began with a scream. I knew that it was a scream of genuine terror, that the person who had unleashed that terrible sound was in mortal danger. I also knew the scream had come from Emily. My heart quickened, a need to find her and keep her safe taking me over. I picked up my pace, adrenalin pushing me on despite my fatigue, legs grazing against claw-like branches as I broke into a run. My right hand held out the torch in front of me, while my left arm shielded my face from injury. The scream came again, louder this time, so I called out. If I could hear Emily, surely she could hear me. My shout was only met with yet another scream, so I pushed on.

My eyes were fixed on the narrow path I was running along, watching out for anything which may trip me over. My torchlight landed on something just ahead, a widening in the path, possibly an exit from the density of the forest. I sped up, desperate to reach something new. It was as I approached the opening that I realised the trees were moving. Just as the path back had become blocked by intertwining branches, the same thing appeared to be happening ahead of me. Was the forest trying to stop me from reaching Emily? I pushed as hard as I could for those last few metres, hitting the wall of branches with as much force as I could muster. They slowed me down, but I had enough momentum to break through, though not without injury.

I fell forward into a clearing, my left arm stinging with cuts and bruises. Rolling on to my back, I glanced at the tree line only to see branches moving towards my ankles, relentless wooden limbs determined to drag me back into their pit. I shuffled away from them, quickly lifting myself to my feet and walked with a limp towards the centre of the clearing. Darkness still prevailed and I was unsure if it was night, or just that this place never saw the sun. However, the darkness was not as suffocating as it had been within the forest, and I could make out the boundaries of the clearing.

I found myself in a square of short grass, each side around one hundred feet in length and surrounded on all four sides by almost black trees with no obvious entry points. I shone my torch around and could see no sign of life. I held my breath, trying desperately to figure out which direction to take in order to find Emily. Silence had descended, even the wind had disappeared. Instinct told me to head to the centre of the clearing to gain a better view. I did not see the opening until I was almost upon it.

169

I managed to save myself from falling, but only just. In what appeared to be the exact centre of the clearing was a hole in the ground, only four feet in diameter and perfectly round. The fact that it was perfectly round suggested that it was man-made, or at least not just a sinkhole. That was the logic I used, despite nothing else in this dreamland making any sense. I searched around the clearing for another way but knew it would be futile. That hole, tunnel, trap, whatever it was, would be the only way to go. I felt the fear gripping me once again, the knowledge that this was merely a dream doing little to stop my heart racing, and I used my torch to illuminate the passage.

The light could not penetrate far enough to see the bottom, but wooden blocks jutted out of the earth on one side, so I lowered myself in. Each step felt slick with damp and mud and the risk of falling felt all too real. I managed to wedge the torch into one of my belt loops, so that I could see the steps below, and clung on for dear life as I made my descent, counting the steps as I went. I was sixty steps down when Emily's scream almost caused me to lose my footing. I still could not see the bottom, so I did not dare move any quicker, but my determination to reach her grew stronger yet with that scream.

Seventy steps and still darkness. Eighty and something looked different beneath me. Ninety and I was almost there. One hundred steps exactly and my feet were on solid ground. Too solid perhaps, as I realised that I was standing on concrete. For a moment I thought there was nowhere to go, that perhaps this was a disused well, but the darkness had disguised a most certainly man-made tunnel. After praising myself again for bringing the torch, I took a hesitant step inside. Another scream. The time for being afraid was over. So what if I died in a dream, Emily was taking too long to get to. I decided to run.

Aside from the inconvenience of the darkness, the floor was even and easy to run on. Another scream echoed through the tunnel, louder yet again. I kept moving, certain that Emily would be nearby. The tunnel felt endless as I ran and ran, the screams coming more often and more loudly until I found the end. Perhaps 'found' is the wrong word; I came flying through the end of tunnel into a circular room illuminated by hundreds of candles and collided with a figure in a black robe. In the centre of the room was a pillar of solid stone, ornately carved with images of trees, and tied to the pillar stood Emily.

Her pale white arms were stretched behind her, tied together on the other side of the pillar. Her face was red and blotchy, eyes puffy from crying, and yet she still looked beautiful. The red cape and hood outfit was short, revealing her legs in all their glory. Alabaster skin now coated in dry blood from scratches, her bare feet now swollen and stained crimson. The forest had not been kind to her either.

"Emily!" I shouted, but there was no reply. She did not even look at me, her eyes transfixed on one of the candles. She was oblivious of my presence, but the figure in the robe was not. He turned to face me, and I shoved him, but in my weakened state it was not enough to knock him off his feet. He lunged towards me, throwing me against the wall. I tried to see beneath the hood, but all I could make out was a mask of some kind, a wolf, perhaps. He landed several hard blows to my stomach and I dropped.

Weakly, I called out to Emily again. Nothing.

My attacker brought his leg up, causing his booted foot to connect with my jaw and sending a tooth flying from my mouth. I tasted blood, I saw my Emily in distress, and I lost it. I was consumed by a rage, the likes of which I have never felt before. As the figure swung his leg towards me again, I grabbed it, toppling him over. Before I even knew what I was doing, I was on top of him, my hands around his throat. I could feel him begin to weaken so I lifted my right hand and removed the wolf mask. It took a few seconds for my sleep-deprived mind to process what I was seeing and, when it did, I fell back in horror.

"Who are you?" I asked, my voice barely audible. I already knew the answer, I was sure of it, but I needed to hear it from this thing, this monster. "Why do you wear my face?" I demanded.

"You're wearing my face," it countered. "My old face." I didn't understand at all, causing my frustration to grow.

"You're not making any fucking sense!" I yelled. "Why can't Emily see or hear me? What have you done to her?"

"Metaphors," I was told. "What don't you understand? You seemed to follow the first two dreams perfectly well." I thought back to them, and he was right.

"Emily was there, running away from me, just like in real life. But this is completely different."

"Not really. You just continued chasing her. You were persistent. Some women might find that flattering, but Emily didn't. She wanted to be left alone, to be free of you. Of us. *We* chased her relentlessly. The screaming only started when *we* caught up with her, took her back, made her ours again. We will never stop chasing her until we win her back, but it isn't what she wants."

"So..." I began slowly, trying to analyse this bizarre dream, "you're saying that if I keep chasing her then we'll be together again? But she won't be happy?"

"That's for sure."

"But," I continued, "I haven't even tried to contact her for weeks. I've sorted myself out, I'm trying to move on."

"You really don't see it, do you? All this self-improvement you've been patting yourself on the back about, it's all for her. You think if you quit drinking, work out a

174

bit, she'll come back. And she will. But when she does, you'll revert back to the nasty bastard you were when she was there."

"I wouldn't do anything to ruin a second chance like that," I protested.

"But you will. I'm you and you're me. I know what happens and it isn't pretty. There is only one way to prevent that from happening."

"Which is?" I asked, already knowing the answer.

"You have to die."

***

I woke up in a mess; my hands shook, my breathing shallow, bedsheets soaked through once again. It had been all too real. I glanced at the clock to find it was almost midday. *Too late for work,* I decided, and made my way to the kitchen in search of coffee. Passing the front door, I noticed the larger-than-usual pile of post. *Coffee first.* I turned my phone on, ready to sound ill as I called my employer. The manager answered on the third ring and I went into my spiel about feeling sick last night and how I must have slept through my alarm. I told him I was sorry for not calling earlier.

"I should think so too!" he replied. "If you are sick then you need to let us know straightaway, not the next bloody week! Get yourself sorted and be here tomorrow or I'll be taking action." The phone went dead. My mind began racing, the dream still clear in my head, the voyage through the forest which had felt like days of walking. I looked at the screen on my mobile and didn't believe it. I switched on the small TV in the kitchen and checked the listings. Finally, I moved to the front door and picked up the free paper from the pile on the mat. Five days had passed.

Everything came to me all at once, everything that the wolf-mask wearing version of me had said. Was it only a dream? I've never heard of anyone sleeping for that long. And would Emily come back to me? Would I end up hurting her and going through all this again one day? *There's only one way to prevent that from happening.* The words hit me, and I knew the truth behind them.

I took a knife from the block on the kitchen side and lacerated both forearms. A peace came over me in that instant, certain that I had done the best thing for Emily. As blackness took over my vision, I heard the knock at the door. I could just about make out the red hood and gown through the glass pane. *Just in time,* I thought. *I saved you Emily.*

# Six Reasons to Live

There had been rumours of a creature dwelling in the woodland around the coastal village of Seahaven for several years and, while most dismissed it as nonsense, very few dared to venture into the woods after dark. Tales were told of a humanoid figure, sometimes up to eight feet in height and completely covered in hair, roaming amongst the trees at night. Young children whispered about *'the hairy beast and his army of wolves'*. Words like *Sasquatch* and *Bigfoot* were thrown around, but none of these caused offense to Alf; he had come to enjoy being feared. Occasionally, he would hear the youngsters playing about in the fields that bordered the woodland, hear them talking about his 'wolves' and daring one another to enter the forest.

"Wolves," he said with a chuckle, looking down at the six Rottweilers curled in a heap beside the fire. Alf had moved out of the village following the death of his wife almost ten years earlier. Everyone had been sympathetic after Clarissa's accident, but nobody could actually help in any way. She had been his soulmate, his everything, and he simply could not cope without her. On the day of the funeral, once he had completed his duties of greeting people who pretended to be his friends and burying his wife, Alf had made his way deep into the woods with the intention of ending his life. He had attempted to pen a note but knew that an explanation was not needed, and he did not care what anyone thought of his choice. Armed only with a bottle of bourbon and a thick rope, Alf marched through the darkness of the forest in search of the right tree for the job.

He had no doubt that suicide was what he wanted; after all, there was no one worth staying alive for now. They had never had children, and Alf did not care for the company of anyone else from the village. After more than an hour of wandering the muddy trails, most of the bourbon having been consumed on the way, Alf came across the perfect location for his final goodbye. A solid oak tree stood before him, branches thicker than his own arms, and he stared upwards, trying to work out the logistics of the act.

Alf's thoughts were interrupted by a

whimpering which sounded all the louder in the stillness of the forest. The noise was not human, of that Alf was certain, and he cautiously poked about in the shrubbery, expecting to find an injured animal. That was the first time he saw her. Lying on her side and crying, belly bloated to a seemingly impossible size, was a Rottweiler. Alf approached with some hesitation, not wanting to frighten the poor dog, especially as she was in pain and was more likely to become aggressive. Alf watched from a safe distance, unable to offer any assistance, as the Rottweiler produced a litter of six.

Something happened that evening which changed Alf's perspective entirely. He knew that the puppies were unlikely to survive if left in the woods, and now it seemed as if he had a purpose. *Suicide can wait,* he reasoned. *Let's get these little fellas somewhere safe first.* Alf knew that he could not very well pick up six small dogs, even if the mother allowed him to do so. He made his way, somewhat drunken by this time, back to his home to retrieve blankets and a box. It was all he could offer, aside from his company, and decided that it would have to do. Returning to the spot several hours later, after becoming a little lost in the darkness of the trees, Alf covered the dogs with several blankets and curled up on the cold ground beside them to sleep.

Awakening that first morning as the sunlight streamed through the canopy above, Alf felt reborn. There was still an all-encompassing sadness at the loss of Clarissa, but the pull of that final intended act had weakened considerably during the night. Right at that moment, in that place on the ground, was where he felt safe. Alf had no interest in human interaction, no desire for money or other material things. He could think of no reason why he should not just stay where he was. Of course, the people in the village would not understand but Alf did not care. He just needed to figure out the details, grab a few bits from his home, and create his new life on the fringes of society.

Leaving the pups to suckle their mother's milk, Alf made his way back to his home in the early morning light. The streets were virtually deserted at this hour and he saw only a handful of cars on the road. Keen to get back to the forest before he saw anyone he knew, Alf grabbed a large bag and darted from room to room. He threw some clothes into the bag, along with some essentials including a toothbrush, toilet roll, a couple of wedding photographs, and the small amount of food that was still in the fridge. Alf also took a few items of cutlery and crockery from the kitchen, some tins of soup from the cupboard, a torch, and plenty of matches. He knew he could return whenever it became necessary but was determined to avoid this for as long as possible. Loaded with the heavy bag, Alf trudged back into the woods and was relieved to find the litter of pups just as he had left them. And so, he began his new life.

Now, almost ten years later, Alf had returned to his house only a handful of times, and always under the cover of darkness. His disappearance had been a mystery to the townsfolk of Seahaven and may suspected suicide. If anyone had wondered at the connection between Alf's apparent departure and the rare sightings of the creature in the woods, no one spoke of it aloud. Alf was unrecognisable now, his hair falling almost to his waist with his beard not far behind. His skin was wrinkled from age and grimy with dirt from living outdoors. His teeth were yellowed and uncared for. But he was happy. He had spent all these years living among the trees, feeding himself with whatever he could find in the forest. The pups had remained loyal, largely because their mother, whom Alf had named Clarissa, had chosen to follow Alf wherever he would go. The four-legged Clarissa had also passed away several years previously, but Alf was certain this was purely from old age.

Alf never gave names to the Rottweiler puppies, simply numbering them one to six, and after the loss of their mother they never left his side. The dogs were feral, having only ever known life in the wild. They hunted well, catching squirrels, rabbits, and even the occasional badger, and provided enough meat for Alf and the six animals to survive on. Interaction with other humans was successfully avoided. Alf knew every part of the forest and kept out of sight and away from any pathways that other people may use. His dogs knew to stay with their master, and this meant the group had kept out of trouble - until that night.

Alf had heard the scream pierce the darkness. Although he did not know the hour, the temperature was low, and the moon was at its fullest. There had only been the one scream, but it was enough for his six companions to rise to their feet, whimpering quietly as if they were awaiting the order to investigate. Alf waited, expecting to hear another scream, but nothing came.

"Don't worry guys," he whispered. "Probably just some kids mucking about. Best to just keep clear." Alf made himself comfortable on the ground and slowly the six joined him, encircling him as they lay in the mud. The following morning the group began to hunt for their breakfast; Alf gathered blackberries while the dogs scurried about in the brush in search of something meatier to feast upon. The dogs had been trained to be quiet, to only bark when absolutely necessary, not only for the benefit of hunting their prey, but to avoid any confrontations with other humans. When Alf heard the barks that morning, he knew something was very wrong.

Rushing to his pups, shushing them as he approached, Alf nearly vomited when he saw what they had found. The woman was young, perhaps in her late teens, but it was hard to tell through the damage. Next to her head was a rock, glinting red in the early sunlight. Her face had been almost entirely destroyed, cracked white bones jutting through broken skin along her jawline. Her white blouse was torn open, black skirt riding high up her thighs, wrists and ankles bound with tape.

"Jesus Christ," Alf muttered, fighting back a tear. He had heard the scream, quite possibly her last ever sound, and he had not acted. A wave of guilt hit him as he dropped to his knees in the dirt. His six dogs sat, whimpering, in a circle around the corpse. They did not know what to do, and neither did Alf. His first thought had been that he would need to face his fears and head to town; the police needed to be told. However, it did not take long before those words came back to haunt him; he was the *hairy beast with his pack of wolves.* Surely, he would be the prime suspect?

Alf was at a loss. Aside from the tragedy of the young woman's brutal murder, he did not know how to keep himself safe. If he reported the body to the authorities, he was certain they would try to pin it on him. If he pretended not to know about it, simply left the corpse there for someone else to stumble across, he may well end up in the same predicament - a body in the woods would certainly be tied to the crazy man who lived there. The only possibility he could think of was to bury the body, but if he were ever found out then he'd appear even more guilty. *Perhaps it's time we moved on?* he wondered, not knowing where they could go. It took Alf almost two hours to decide what to do, and he did not like it at all.

Not owning a shovel made the job harder than it already was, and Alf cursed the dogs for their lack of assistance. They foraged about in the trees, playing with one another as though the corpse was of no significance to them. Alf supposed that it wasn't, not really. The dogs were wild, and death was just a part of life; they had no comprehension of the trouble that Alf could find himself in if he were to be discovered.

The grave was not deep, barely covering the young woman, but Alf created a layer of branches and leaves to disguise the disturbed ground. He knew the animals of the forest would eventually pick up the scent of rotting flesh and make a mess of the scene, but he viewed this as unavoidable in the long run. All he could hope for was that he would be out of sight and as far from the mess as possible.

Alf and the loyal six spent the day trudging through the forest, almost to its furthest point. He understood the danger he would put himself in if he left the perceived safety of the trees, but he was also determined to put as much distance between himself and the grave as possible. By the time the sun had begun its descent, Alf was exhausted. Food had been more scarce than usual with no time to hunt for meat, leaving the dogs with empty bellies and Alf surviving only on blackberries and a handful of wild mushrooms. Alf led the dogs deep amongst the trees until he found a suitable spot to spend the night. The night was cool, but not uncomfortably cold, and Alf curled up beneath a large ash tree as the dogs collapsed around him.

He had been asleep for little more than an hour before the dogs' whining woke him. Alf could just about make out their shapes in the darkness of night, all six of them stood upright, all facing in the same direction and crying as though afraid. Tufts of black fur stood on end along each of their backs, tails between their legs. Alf's first thought was that the police were coming for him, that his makeshift grave had been discovered. He listened intently through the sounds of the night creatures scurrying about but could hear no voices. *The police would be out in force, they'd be noisy and have lights,* he reasoned, but this did little to ease his mind. *Whoever killed that girl could be back.* The idea of confronting a killer made Alf less nervous than dealing with the police; he had six large dogs who he knew would protect him, and if were able to restrain the killer then perhaps he could even turn him in. *It would be easy enough to say the killer had buried the body,* he reasoned.

Still, Alf could hear no voices, no sound of brittle twigs snapping underfoot, no heavy breathing from a killer's chest. Whatever had gotten the dogs so riled was beyond him, but it couldn't be ignored. Trying to disregard the aches and pains that spread through his body, Alf rose to his feet as quietly as possible.

"What's wrong?" he whispered, only

leading to an increase in the dogs' whining noises. "What have you seen?" His question was greeted with a yelp from one dog, followed by terrifying snarls from the others. Something was coming, something which had changed his usually jolly dogs into something much more volatile. And then he saw it. At first it was a flash of white moving between the trees in complete silence. As soon as he had seen it, it had vanished behind a thick bush. Breath held in the stillness of the forest, Alf's eyes darted back and forth, attempting to locate whatever he had seen. The dogs' snarls had increased in ferocity and Alf knew it was coming closer. A rustle of leaves to his left caught his attention, followed by a white blur passing in front of him. The already cool night dropped suddenly in temperature as the apparition passed him.

The dogs were close to boiling point, desperate to lunge at whatever lie before them yet unable to catch it, foam spraying from their mouths as they released a series of guttural howls. Then they fell silent, as though someone had flicked a switch. The whining and the snarling ceased from each and every one of them at

189

the same instant as they sat on their haunches and turned their attention to Alf. This was the first time that Alf had ever felt afraid of his dogs, the way they all stared at him in unison causing his hands to tremble.

Another shaking of leaves came from behind the dogs, followed by a quick breeze of icy wind, and then she appeared. Alf's bladder released as he gazed upon her, looking just as she had when he had buried her. Aside from being upright, the young woman looked to be in no better condition. Her face, cracked, shattered, and bloody, bore what appeared to be an attempt at a grin. Her white blouse remained open at the front, exposing her dirt-covered bra and torso. The black skirt barely covered her underwear, and Alf spotted the torn remnants of the tape on her wrists and ankles.

"You were dead," Alf managed, barely above a whisper.

"So?" the woman replied. "Did that give you the right to hide me away, to assist my killers?" The words came out oddly through her misshapen mouth and Alf struggled to understand them. What was left of her face showed something akin to

190

anger, but Alf could not bring himself to look at the gruesome mess before him. He prayed that he was merely dreaming, a by-product of guilt perhaps. But it felt all too real.

"I'm sorry," he told her, despite not meaning it. Alf was certain that ghosts did not exist, that whatever this was must surely be a figment of his imagination. For if ghosts did exist, he reasoned, then where was his Clarissa? "What do you want from me?" he asked, keen to end this nightmare. "Do you want me to tell the police what I found? Can you tell me who killed you?"

"My killer is not your concern," she replied. "I have no intention of involving the police; how could I? I will avenge my own death, in my own way. It is not your assistance I seek."

"Then what *do* you want?" Alf asked, fearful of the answer. The apparition did not speak, simply pointing at the six creatures before her. "You want my dogs?" Alf asked, the surprise in his voice evident.

"*Your* dogs?" she replied angrily. "They belong to the earth; they owe you nothing." At that, the six rose to their feet, eyes still set on Alf, a snarl rising from

191

each of them.

"I have loved them since they were born!" Alf stated, tears welling in his eyes. "They kept me alive, gave me a purpose. I can't lose them now."

"It's too late for that. Consider it your penance for what you did to me."

"Then take me with you," Alf pleaded. "I don't want to be alone." He broke down into full sobs, dropping to the ground among the dried leaves and dirt.

"Perhaps you should revisit your original plan, Alfred," the apparition told him, her voice dripping with menace. "You know, the one with the rope and the tree." He did not answer, that very thought having already come to him at the idea of being left alone. "But don't get any ideas about a romantic reunion, Clarissa isn't waiting for you." The sobs came to a sudden halt at the mention of his wife and he stared up at the monster before him. Did Clarissa remain somewhere, on some plane of existence?

"You've spoken to her?" Alf asked, desperate to know where Clarissa now was.

"I can sense her," she said, her voice void of any sympathy. "She doesn't want anything to do with you."

"Liar!" Alf yelled. "If you're here then she must be somewhere, why hasn't she shown herself?"

"Perhaps she wanted you to move on with your life? You really think she'd want to spend the afterlife in this dingy forest?"

"I could never move on," Alf admitted. "She was my everything, all I ever wanted. When she died, I so badly wanted to go with her. If I'd known she still existed in some form, then I would have joined her years ago." Alf stood himself back up, a resolute look on his face. "You're not taking my dogs," he said, his face etched in determination.

"You have no choice," the apparition said, pointing to a branch above Alf's head. From it hung a noose of new-looking rope. He shook his head before taking a step towards the dogs. Their usual excited wagging of tails was replaced by angry snarls, but Alf took another step. The dogs matched his steps, closing the gap between them.

As Alf reached out a hand towards his companions, they launched at him, the ghostly apparition taking full control of her hellhounds. Alf focussed his mind on his wife, hoping beyond all hope that he would be able to find her on the other side. As teeth tore into his throat, Alf let out a gargled cry. "Clarissa, I'm coming."

# I Lived For Too Long

I have a set route for running. I say it's set, but it does allow for few options to alter the distance depending on my level of motivation. The route I refer to as standard comes in at a little over five kilometres, but if I take a later turn off then I can bump this up to seven. I couldn't say how many times I'd run this route over the last few years, but it must be into the hundreds.

It can be a brutal course in the winter months, with its narrow, muddy tracks and steep inclines. Obscured rabbit holes have taken me down a few times. If the wind is strong, and blowing to the south, it adds an element of danger as the track passes mere inches from the cliff edge. Danger, as always, comes with excitement.

On *that* Sunday morning in early June, 2017, the sky was clear. I had expected it to be a warm day so left for my run a little earlier than usual, my wife and daughter still dozing. My biggest regret, aside from even leaving the house that day, is not waking them to say goodbye.

Pulling on my running shoes, I closed the front door quietly, so as not to disturb them. I remember feeling fresh and motivated as I tapped my watch to begin recording my distance, deciding to take the longer version of my route. Sunday mornings in my small town were often quiet and I only passed one other person in the first five minutes of my run.

As much as I enjoyed the route, the first part of it was a hard slog uphill and I always needed to take a moment on reaching the summit. Having meandered through the streets leading to the country track and followed it up to the expanse of green, I paused for a minute or so to catch my breath. Slowly jogging to the other side of the field, amidst the chatter of birds, I checked my watch out of habit to confirm this was still the one-kilometre mark.

From there, the gravel path winds at a slight incline until it reaches an intersection of sorts; the left turn takes me down to the cliff edge and along my five kilometre route, straight on takes me around in a loop for the longer distance. I decided to pass the turning, as I was jogging comfortably, and followed the gravel path as it made its descent into the neighbouring town. I muttered a 'good morning' to an elderly dog walker who I'd seen many times along there and he tipped his Fedora in greeting, the puppy pulling him in every direction.

196

Looking back, I can't explain what made me take a different turning. Perhaps there was something pulling me that way, but I don't recall it being a conscious decision. I knew the route so well that I could have drawn a map detailing each change in gradient, each narrowing of the trail, and each one-kilometre point along it. I had never noticed that turning, however.

On my descent along the gravel path, to where it joins with a proper road, I turned to the right. I always turn to the right, but this path was a little earlier than my usual turn. Not putting much thought into it, I had assumed it would meet the path I needed to be on. Then it hit me.

In an instant everything changed. My warm, sweat-drenched body broke out in goose bumps. The clear skies immediately darkened, within a fraction of a second, and I found myself in the middle of a downpour. This was no sudden change in the weather – there had not been a cloud in the sky. It took me a few steps to reach a stop and I turned where I stood. Behind me everything looked normal, aside from the complete alteration in weather.

I checked my distance, seeing that I was approaching the three-kilometre mark. Nothing seemed off about that, but I didn't fancy the muddy trails so close to the cliff edge in this rain. I turned back, retracing my steps. The rain was relentless, my body beginning to shiver with the cold. I pushed on, determined to get home as quickly as possible and get into a hot shower. I remember wondering what my wife had made of the freak storm, for that was all I could come up with as an explanation.

When I was almost back to the field, I spotted the elderly man again. This time a black umbrella kept his Fedora dry, his dog still pulling at him. I managed a smile as I passed him, but it was only a moment or two later that my mind began to process what I had seen. It was certainly the same man I had passed many times, the same man I'd greeted less than half an hour ago. There was no doubt in my mind that he hadn't been carrying an umbrella earlier. *Had he gone home to collect it?* That was possible, but the dog....

Was my mind playing tricks on me? Had I only glanced at the animal from an angle, mistaking it for a puppy? For it was certainly not a puppy now, but rather a full-grown dog. My thoughts, and subsequent confusion, kept me ploughing on until I reached my front door. From there on, things went from baffling to terrifying.

I don't take anything out with me when I run, despite my wife's nagging about needing my phone for when I inevitably injure myself. I especially don't take my keys and I *always* leave the door unlocked for when I return. I rushed to the door, pushed down the handle and collided with the wet metal. Frustrated, I pressed the doorbell, waiting rather impatiently for an answer.

I couldn't fathom why my wife would have locked up, unless she'd needed to go out, but that would imply an emergency of some kind. Then my confusion turned to panic as I thought of my daughter, wondering if something had happened to necessitate a hospital trip with me being unreachable due to my stubborn refusal to take my phone out with me. That line of thought was cut off quickly by a key turning in the lock.

I took a step forward as soon as the door began to open but was stopped in my tracks by the man standing there. A little older than me, as well as a little taller, his face registered anger at my presence. My mind darted to a place I didn't want it to go but I quickly took a hold of it. My wife had been sleeping when I left – the chance of her waking up and calling another man over early on a Sunday morning, knowing

199

I'd only be gone for forty minutes or so, was absurd.

"Who the hell are you?" the man asked, looking as though I'd woken him up.

"I live here!" I said, glaring at him, no reasonable explanation coming to mind.

"Nah," the man replied, "you got the wrong house." Shaking his head, he started to close the door and I jammed my sodden trainer in the gap before it could shut completely. "The fuck you think you're doing?" he growled.

"This is my house," I said again. "I don't know what you're doing here but *I* live here, with my wife and daughter." Before the man could reply I saw movement behind him, a chubby woman appearing as she pulled her dressing gown closed.

"What's going on?" she asked, tiptoeing to see over the man's shoulder.

"He says he lives here, tried to come inside." I stood, speechless, as the couple laughed amongst themselves.

"But..." I began, feebly.

"No buts. Now piss off before I call the police," the man said, angry eyes flicking from my face to my shoe and back again. I pulled my foot from beside the doorframe and watched the door click shut. The rain wasn't letting up, but adrenalin was now keeping me warm. I made my way to the house next to mine, searching for answers.

When Pauline, the woman who had been my neighbour for over seven years, opened the door to me she screamed. I watched her eyes widen, her jaw fall slack, and then the silence of the street was shattered. She backed away from the open door slowly, screaming as she took each step.

I acted without thought, stepping into Pauline's home and closing the door behind me. I was certain that the couple who appeared to have taken over my home would have heard the screams and I expected them to come knocking within minutes.

"Pauline," I said, trying to keep my voice friendly. "It's me. From next door. What's wrong?" The screams gradually turned to a whimper as she slid to the floor in her hallway. "Pauline," I repeated, crouching down to her level and avoiding getting too close. I watched as she tried to regulate her breathing, thoughts firing rapidly behind her eyes.

"I thought you were dead," she said. "Everyone thought you were dead."

"I don't understand," I replied, honestly. "Why would you think I was dead? I came round to see if you knew why there were people in my house. I left my phone behind but I'm going to need to call the police."

"Yes, the police," Pauline muttered, pulling herself up. "The police can help." I watched as she made her way into the living room and lifted the receiver on her landline.

"Who are those people in my house?" I asked, my hands trembling.

"Frank and Sue," Pauline replied. "They've lived there for five years." My mind raced, pieces of information falling into place like some horrific jigsaw puzzle. The sudden change in weather, the puppy becoming a dog, new tenants in my house, Pauline's shock.

"Pauline," I said, my voice shaking. "Where are Maddie and Elizabeth? Where is my family?" I watched Pauline's fingers hover over the numbers, as though deciding whether to call the police just yet.

"Come and sit down," she told me. "I'll get you a towel and something hot to drink."

***

"Six years," Pauline said. "Well, it'll be six years in June. That's when you disappeared."

"But it *is* June," I said, unconvinced by my own words.

"It's March. March, 2023." Pauline flung a newspaper at me and I stared in disbelief – *March 16th, 2023.*

"And Maddie?" I asked, desperately trying to hold back the tears.

"She was devastated, of course," Pauline explained. "Had the police and coastguard searching for you for weeks. Eventually, they decided you must have fallen from the cliff and been swept out to sea." The thought of my wife and daughter thinking I was dead was too much to bear and the tears came with earnest, building up to great, heaving sobs of despair. "I guess there were too many memories in that house. They moved six months after that."

"I need to find them," I said. For me, it had been an hour since leaving the house, but so much could have changed for Maddie in six years, even more so for Elizabeth who was only three. Pauline didn't look at me, her gaze fixed to a spot on the carpet. "What is it?" I asked.

"Six years is a long time," she said. "Things have changed. You can't just run off without a word for all this time and expect to walk back into their lives."

"I didn't run off!" I almost shouted. "I left the house, *my* house, an hour ago. If you know where Maddie is then please tell me so I can sort this all out."

"America," Pauline said softly, slowly lifting her gaze to meet mine. With that one word I felt everything fall apart. I didn't need to hear more; my wife and daughter had started a new life on the other side of the world, maybe she had even remarried. I had no means of doing anything about it either – no phone, no money, not even dry clothes. All I could think to do was to return to the place where everything had changed.

I mumbled a 'thanks' to Pauline and walked out of the house. The rain had eased up, but it was still too cold for comfort. Attempting to bring some warmth to my body, I repeated my run from earlier (whether that was an hour ago or almost six years ago, I couldn't say), not even stopping for breath in my usual spot. Part of me feared that the turning, that fateful path to whatever this hell is, would no longer be there. My fears were put to rest when I saw it, however, and I took a few steps off to the right before stopping.

There was no indication of any change approaching but I guess I had been a few metres along the track when the weather had changed so suddenly. I had returned here due to a lack of options, but now that

I stood in this place I had to pause. Assuming that this amount of time had passed, that I had somehow jumped forward almost six years, what would happen if I continued along this path? Would I then find myself in the year 2029? Would nothing happen at all? If I approached from the other end of the trail, would it take me back? I so desperately wanted to go back that I felt the tears begin to flow again as I realised I had already turned back that morning. Whatever this thing was, I'd passed through from the other side and nothing had changed.

Steadying myself, I walked forward, slowly taking a step at a time. For a moment I thought nothing was going to happen but then it did. There was no drastic change in weather this time, but the sky flickered, turning a little darker than it had been. There was a noticeable drop in temperature, a subtle alteration in the size of the surrounding grasses and flowers, but nothing more.

*Colder,* I thought. *June 2017 to March 2023, five years and nine months. If it's worked the same way then it's December 2028.* Lacking the energy to return to Pauline, I chose to knock on one of the few remote houses nearby. There was no answer from any until I knocked on the fourth house, a large, detached property in need of maintenance.

As soon as I had pressed the bell, I could sense movement inside and heard the weak bark of a dog. I watched through the frosted glass of the door as a hunched figure approached, struggling to pull the door open. I recognised him immediately, even without the Fedora. An old dog stumbled up behind its master.

"Can I help you?" the man asked, squinting up at me.

"I'm very sorry to disturb you," I began. "This is going to sound like the strangest question, but can you tell me the date?"

"I recognise you," the man replied, not answering my question. "You used to come running along here almost every day."

"Uh, yes, I did."

"You don't look a day older," he said, looking me up and down.

"Please, sir, I just need to know the date."

"It's New Year's Eve," the old man said with a bemused smile. "Do you need to know the year too?"

"Please," I said.

"2028." Despite the absurdity, I congratulated myself at having guessed correctly.

"Thank you," I muttered before turning away. I heard the man mumbling something as he closed the door, but I couldn't make out the words. I weighed up what I already knew, no doubt left in my mind now. Whatever was down that trail, whether it could be called a portal, a tear in time, or whatever, it always moved me forward by the same amount of time. It's impossible to go through it the other way so that wouldn't be the way back. These facts left me with the all-important question: where is the portal to take me home?

*** 

I wandered aimlessly for days. Having no family or anyone else I could trust meant I had nowhere to go for help, or at least for some dry clothes. The police had been tempting, but I knew they couldn't really help, and I'd probably end up in more trouble. I genuinely feared they would lock me away in some asylum.

When faced with the reality of my situation, I would have preferred to hunt down a needle in a barn-sized haystack. It didn't take me long to give up my search for an invisible portal which could be anywhere in the world, if it even existed.

And if I were to stumble upon it there was no guarantee where, or rather *when*, it would take me to. This left me with three options – track down Maddie and Elizabeth in America, eleven and half years after my 'death' and hope they would take me in, try to rebuild my life here with no money and no identity, or just keep running through the portal.

The second option wasn't going to work, I'd known that from the start. It wasn't simply a case of finding a job or gaining access to my bank account and credit cards. Everything was gone – I no longer existed. This lack of identity made the possibility of tracking down my family close enough to zero. I could not travel to the States, I had no way of tracking them down; Maddie may even have a different surname by now. The hopelessness of it all hit me once again and I broke down in tears on a lonely part of the beach where I had been sleeping. Suicide was tempting; I'd lost everything, had no money, no future, and was on the verge of starving to death. But I had the opportunity to see the future, for as long as that portal remained. I had felt it calling me from the day I'd left the house in June and I knew that was where I needed to be.

***

I walked through, casually; I was actually thankful the portal was still there. As with the last time, there were only subtle differences in sky colour, plant life, and temperature. I turned back, re-entered the pathway, and walked through the portal again. It was evident I was travelling through the seasons and I remained confident that the same amount of time was passing with each 'trip'. I began to run, paying no attention to the changes around me as I went through the portal, over and again, until I'd lost count of the number of times. Judging by my level of exhaustion as I slumped to the ground, I'd guess at having run four or five kilometres in my state of malnutrition. Estimating the distance back and forth I may have passed through around a thousand times. I tried to guess at the year, but it was beyond me as I lay there, the sun still shining as though all were well with the world.

Pulling myself into a sitting position, I surveyed the area. Those subtle changes I had experienced previously had combined into huge differences. The cliff edge was now far closer as coastal erosion had taken its toll. There was no sign of the houses which had stood along this gravel path, not even ruins. In fact, the path itself had been reclaimed by nature.

I began to walk, the long grass I now found myself in almost coming to my waist. The main road was gone, or at least fully buried beneath the greenery, as were the buildings which had previously formed the town I was entering. There was only luscious green in every direction. My stomach rumbled and I chuckled out loud. It had been three days since I had eaten, but it had also been thousands of years. No wonder I was hungry!

I hiked, feeling as though I were exploring some far-off jungle, until I reached a part of the coastline which naturally dipped to sea level. From there I wandered the rocky beaches, picking at cockles and muscles, swallowing them down raw. I sat, remarkably content, staring out to sea and wondering if I was the last human alive. Until the roar of the helicopter broke my reverie.

***

I use the word helicopter because that was what the mechanical beast reminded me most of, but it was unlike anything I'd ever seen. Even the writers of futuristic movies and books hadn't conjured up anything quite like this. It approached from behind me and must have been travelling at some speed as it was on top of me as soon as I'd registered the sound. I looked up, staring partly in awe and partly in terror.

Whilst it bore a slight resemblance to a military helicopter in shape, it moved in a way that looked almost alive. The tail appeared to swish in the air, like that of an angry cat. The main body of the craft was near spherical, entirely black, and I could make out no entry point or even windows. Perhaps a flying, metallic tadpole would be a better description.

There was nothing friendly about this craft, that much was obvious, but I had nowhere to hide on this open stretch of beach. The machine hovered above me as I waited, and I knew if I tried to run it wouldn't end well. The roar that it was emitting changed in frequency, its deep rumbling becoming more high-pitched. The sound was reaching an unbearable level and, just when I thought my eardrums would rupture, the sound stopped completely. At least, I perceived it as having stopped but it may well have reached a frequency beyond my comprehension, like a dog whistle.

The silence was eerie as that thing seemed to float barely ten feet above me. My heart raced as I sat, eyes fixed on the underbelly of the machine, waiting for something, anything, to happen. What felt like full minutes passed as I sat transfixed, until a scream of 'Run!' snapped me out of it.

Further up the beach I saw two people, ragged and dirty but armed. The man was aiming a large weapon at the craft above me and I wasted no time scrambling to my feet. Whoever, or whatever, was inside that machine must have sensed the danger and the air was again filled with a sudden roar. I watched as a rocket was fired towards the black metal, the craft failing to respond in time. The snake-like tail exploded as the rocket found its target, sending the rest of the craft spiralling into the rocky ground, mere feet from where I stood. I expected a further explosion, one that would take me with it, but the ruined metal carcass simply fizzled to a stop.

I stood, unsure what move to make. The pair were armed, so running was futile. They had, possibly, just saved me from whatever that thing was.

"What the hell were you doing?" the

woman shouted as they came closer. "Have you got a death wish?"

"What is that thing?" I replied, my question met with dumbfounded looks.

"Where did you come from?" the man asked me, eyeing me up and down. "We haven't seen any other humans around here for years. How did you get all the way down to the coast undetected?"

"I've always lived around here," I replied, not wanting to go into any more detail.

"Bullshit," the man said, unholstering a pistol and pointing it at me. "It didn't look like you'd even seen one of those things before. No way you could have survived this long on your own."

I studied the pair for a moment. They were frightened, that much was clear. But afraid and armed didn't make a good combination and I had no interest in making friends. I turned to leave.

"You're welcome," the woman shouted at my back. I paused.

"For what?" I asked.

"Oh, I don't know, saving your life, perhaps!"

"How do I know that thing was any more likely to hurt me than you guys?" I replied with a shrug. The woman looked incredulous. The man levelled the pistol at my face.

"You need to start talking," he demanded. I thought about it briefly before answering but decided to go with the truth. I didn't especially care if they believed me or not.

"In the year 2017 I found a portal, some kind of rip in time. I went through it, accidentally, and I'd gone almost six years into the future. My family thought I'd died, my wife and daughter had left the country." I tried to keep my voice even but the sadness in it was unmistakable. "I searched for a way back but never found it. In the end, I ran through that damn portal over and over until I could run no more. That's where I'm from. Or rather, *when* I'm from."

I was visibly upset, and I knew what I was saying was the truth, so I'd hoped to be believed. There was a moment of silence as the pair looked at one another.

"Prove it," the woman said. "Where is this portal?"

"Back that way," I said, pointing east. "Maybe five miles or so."

"Take us to it," the man demanded, and I knew he wasn't going to just let me walk away.

***

214

The couple barely spoke as we traversed the thick vegetation. They seemed deep in concentration, listening out for any sounds which could indicate danger. I wanted to ask about the strange craft they had destroyed, and I probably had a million other questions if I took the time to think about it, but it didn't feel like the right time.

I wondered if passing through the portal would create a change large enough for them to even notice. I wondered what would happen if we couldn't find it and how they would react. I soon discovered there were bigger things to worry about.

We began to climb as the terrain rose with the shape of the cliffs and I knew we were close. I muttered that we were near, the woman nodding from her position in front of me. I heard the whoosh of grass behind me, as though something had passed through it at speed. For a moment, I thought the man with the gun to my back had ran off, until I heard a gurgle.

The woman must have heard the same thing as she turned quicker than I did, her scream reaching my ears before I could take in the sight. The man still stood but was unmoving aside from his trembling hands at his sides. His face and torso were a mess of red ribbons, as if someone had taken a box cutter to him, over and over. I watched his bulging eyes as they seemed to plead with me to save him, but it was too late. He dropped to the ground, buried in the long grass, and the woman screamed again.

Now it was my turn to yell 'Run!' and I shoved her forward. She hesitated but only for a fraction of a second.

"What did that?" I asked as we pushed through the greenery.

"Spawn," she said. When I didn't reply, she elaborated. "Like the thing on the beach but much smaller."

"I still don't understand," I said, "But you can tell me later. We need to get to the portal." I heard another whooshing sound and risked a look over my shoulder. She was right, they looked just like the craft on the beach, only these ones were about a foot in length. A group of six were coming up behind us quickly, looking like angry tadpoles. The turning was just ahead so I grabbed the woman's arm and yanked her to the left.

"I don't see anything," she said, her voice filled with panic. I ignored her, almost dragging her along next to me. The sound behind us built up and I thought for a moment the portal had gone, or I'd taken the wrong turning. The change in the weather was slight but I knew we'd passed through. The angry sound behind us hadn't faded, however, and I scolded myself for my stupidity. I had no idea why I'd thought the portal would save us with those creatures so close behind us – they had simply followed us through.

They were on us in seconds, their twitching tails revealing razor-sharp edges. There was no escape, no mercy, no doubt that this world belonged to them now. Humanity had run its course and was no longer top of the food chain. I felt the warmth of spilled blood as I batted at my attackers, more out of reflex than believing it would actually help. Each strike of a tail stung like a thousand paper cuts and I dropped to the wet grass, surrendering to nature, accepting that I'd overstayed my welcome by thousands of years.

# Passing Through

It was a routine trip. I had travelled those roads every weekend, making the fifty-minute journey after work on a Friday evening and returning on a Sunday afternoon. My weekends were filled with fun, two glorious days spent with Jenny before the repetitive routine of office work kicked back in. I had made it safely to her flat on the Friday and, as the weather had been appalling, we had spent the entire weekend in bed, watching television, eating junk food, and making love. Sunday arrived with its usual feelings of sadness; I didn't want to leave, and Jenny did not want me to either, yet neither of us had the courage to suggest we get a place together. If only I'd taken that step earlier, then things could have been very different.

The icy gusts and almost apocalyptic rain had not let up when it came time for me to depart and, after hugging and kissing Jenny goodbye, I dashed out to my car. I was wet through before I even took my seat, frantically getting the heating on and attempting to clear the windows of condensation. I flicked the headlights on, turned the wipers to max, and cautiously edged out of the parking area. I took the drive slow, I'm not an idiot, so I'm quite sure that what happened was not my fault.

Around twenty minutes into the drive home, along a dual carriageway, there is a tunnel to pass through. I remember thinking that the weather must have knocked out the power as the strip-lighting along the roof of the tunnel was off. This had worried me a little, causing me to slow as I entered the tunnel's blackened mouth. Then it happened, and it's difficult to describe exactly as the memory is rather hazy.

I recall entering the tunnel. I don't remember seeing any other cars on the road at that point. There was a flash of light, so brilliant that I was certain I'd lose control of the car and plough into the concrete walls of the tunnel. My eyes opened and I was, miraculously, still on the road, maintaining my course. Only everything had changed.

I sped through the end of the tunnel, not into torrential rain and inky darkness, but into the bright sunlight of a summer's afternoon. My wipers were scraping against the dry windscreen noisily, the light on the dash confirming that my headlights were still switched on. There were no other cars around, but there was also nowhere to safely stop so I continued on my way, increasing my speed in desperation to find a rest stop.

Nothing made sense. My initial thought, as ludicrous as it sounds, was that there had simply been a break in the weather. That in those few seconds I had spent underground, the wind had dropped, and the rain had cleared. Unlikely, but not impossible. Darkness turning to light, however, made no sense. Winter afternoons at this time of year were gloomy enough to have the streetlights coming on; clear skies and sunlight were out of the question. I glanced at the clock on my dashboard, briefly wondering if I had left Jenny at an earlier time than I had realised but saw that it was still late afternoon. Feeling uncomfortable, I pulled into the slip lane and came to a stop at the services car park.

Shutting off the engine, I realised the strangeness of the empty car park. I had only stopped here once or twice, usually for fuel, but had never seen it completely empty before. I exited the car, approaching the fuel station, only to find the door locked and nobody inside despite the 'Open 24/7' sign on the window. The only other amenities were a car wash, also seemingly abandoned, and a coffee shop. I surmised that no cars in the car park meant there would be no customers in the coffee shop and feared that it would also be closed. A wave of relief swept over me as the automatic door slid open on my approach.

My logic was proved correct as I stared at the empty tables - no customers. However, unlike the fuel station, I saw a staff member, his back to me as he cleaned the coffee machine. As I took steps towards the counter, my shoes clicking on the laminate flooring, he spun around and greeted me with a broad grin.

"Hey there!" he declared in a European accent I couldn't quite place. "What can I get you?"

"A flat white," I replied without thinking. "Where is everybody?"

"Just you today," I was told over the sound of the coffee machine. "It's a quiet one, thankfully."

"Just me?" I queried. "All day?" I glanced at the man's name badge as he handed me my coffee. *Charon. Sounds like Sharon,* I thought to myself, grateful that I did not have a feminine sounding name.

"Just you. Can I get you anything else?" Charon asked.

"No," I said slowly.

"Are you okay?"

221

"Sorry," I mumbled. "It's been a really odd day." I felt an urge to explain everything to this man but knew I would sound insane so turned to take a seat by the window.

"I'm sure it has," he replied as I walked away.

Once I had made myself comfortable by the window, gazing out into what looked like a summer's afternoon, I pulled my phone from my pocket. I needed to call Jenny, to talk to someone about where I was, to at least find out if the rain had stopped where she was. No signal. *Shit!* I called out to Charon who was half-heartedly wiping down the tables which had not even been used.

"Do you have a pay phone here? I've got no signal." Charon just laughed before walking away, shaking his head. I muttered a few obscenities under my breath and chose to finish my coffee before searching for a phone myself. I thanked Charon and left the coffee shop, making my way past the fuel station and finding a pay phone in the corner of the car park. Fumbling for some change, I lifted the receiver only to find that the line was dead. I slammed it back down and marched towards the coffee shop. I'd use

Charon's own phone if it came to it.

"Found the pay phone but it's dead," I announced as I re-entered the shop.

"Well, of course it is," Charon replied.

"Can I use the shop phone? Or yours, maybe? I can pay for the call."

"I don't own a phone," he replied. "And the shop doesn't have one either, I'm afraid." Still he managed to keep that wide grin in place.

"I don't believe you," I retorted, "but fine. I'll wait until I'm home then." I stormed out of the shop and headed to my car. Or, more accurately, where my car had been. Now the car park was truly empty. The keys were still in my pocket and I had seen nobody around aside from Charon. Almost walking into the automatic door as I misjudged the speed at which it opened, I returned to Charon and found myself close to angry tears. "My car's been stolen!" I shouted, looking around as if the answer to my problems could be found.

"I'm sorry to hear that, sir," Charon said, that grin beginning to put me on edge.

"Well, what do I do?" I pleaded. "No car, no phones anywhere. No people aside from you. Am I going to have to walk to the nearest town to get help?"

"Don't be so silly," Charon told me. "I need to close up, and then I can give you a ride to wherever you need to go." This offer of generosity made me a little uncomfortable, but I had little choice but to accept.

"I didn't see any other cars," I told him. "Are you parked around the back?"

"Something like that," he told me, confusing me further. I waited by the door until Charon had finished with the closing procedure and we left the coffee shop. He led me around the back of the building, to what looked like a garage. Upon opening the large, barn-like doors, I could see sacks of coffee beans, piles of napkins, and disposable cups, all spread around the edges of the building. In the centre was a brand-new, shiny black Mustang.

"This is yours?" I asked, genuinely shocked that an assistant at a coffee shop could afford something like this. Charon nodded with pride as he unlocked the car.

"Jump in," he ordered, and I did as I was told. "Now, before we leave, I'll need you to give me a few coins for the journey." I took this as a request for some fuel money which had been worded strangely due to English not being his native tongue, and I passed him a note from my wallet. He shook his head. "Coins, please."

I was about to reason that the few coins I had in my pocket would not cover much fuel in a car like this but went along with his request. He took three coins from my hand, winked at me, and started the engine.

"I live about half an hour from here," I began, as we left the car park and pulled on to the eerily empty main road. Charon kept his gaze fixed on the road ahead, ignoring me, pushing the car to go faster. I glanced at the speedometer as it crept past eighty miles per hour. "You need to take the next right," I said but the car maintained its course. Panic began to set it. I was in a car with a stranger heading in the wrong direction. I yelled at him to stop but he gave no response. The car edged over ninety and I was too afraid to grab at Charon, fearing we would crash. "Where are we going?" I shouted.

Suddenly Charon hit the brakes, turning the wheel quickly to take a corner that had appeared out of nowhere. The tyres screeched as the rear of the car skidded into the turn. I managed to read the signpost as we turned: River Styx 1 Mile. My mind raced to place that name, certain that I had heard it before, but I never knew it was nearby. The Mustang lurched forward as it straightened out, travelling at breakneck speed towards the riverbank.

"We're going to crash!" I shouted, certain of the impending doom. The river became closer with each second until we were upon it, Charon showing no sign of slowing the vehicle. I closed my eyes without thinking, ready for the inevitable splash of water. In fact, I heard a series of splashes as I felt my stomach lurch. Not the sound of a car hitting water at high speed and sinking, but the sound of wheels almost skimming across the water's surface like a stone. When I opened my eyes, we were back on the road, the speedometer creeping back up to ridiculous speeds. The road tuned to track, throwing up dust and gravel, before changing again. I felt the repeated thud-thud-thud of wooden planks underneath the car as we made our way across a rickety bridge. A bridge over a river that the signage called 'River Acheron'.

By this point I was convinced that Charon and I would be killed in a smash very soon, and if not then he must have sinister intentions for kidnapping me in this way. I was therefore not prepared when the Mustang came to a sudden stop on the far side of the River Acheron.

"What on earth are you doing?" I yelled, unclipping my seatbelt. "You could have killed us! And where are we? I don't know this place at all. I'm done with this. I'll find my own way." I opened the passenger door and stepped out of the car. Charon stayed where he was. I looked around, trying to ascertain which direction to begin walking in. Ahead of me a storm appeared to be forming; threatening black clouds filled the sky and the rumbles of thunder could just about be made out. I turned around, opting for heading back the way we had come, only to find the bridge over the Acheron now completely destroyed. I opened the door to the Mustang, feeling helpless and afraid.

"Charon," I began. "Where do I go?"

"There is only one way for you to go, my friend," he told me, and for the first time he was not wearing that grin. "This is as far as I can take you."

"I don't understand," I replied, resuming my position in the car.

"Oh, but I think you do. You just need to remember."

"Remember what?" I asked, frustrated that I could not make sense of my situation, or fully understand why the words were so familiar.

"I'm the Ferryman," Charon told me.

There was a moment of total silence before it hit me, everything melding together and bringing bile to my mouth. *My name is Charon...give me a few coins for the journey...cross the rivers Styx and Acheron.*

"I'm dead," I whispered. "And you're taking me to Hades?"

"That's right, my friend."

"How?" I asked, fighting back tears at the thought of not seeing Jenny again.

"The tunnel. You hit the wall. You remember a flash of light?" I nodded. "That wasn't the 'light guiding you to heaven' or any of that nonsense. That was the high beams of a truck behind you which rammed you off the road."

"I was murdered?" This news shocked me almost as much as discovering I was dead. "Do you know who by?"

"I do. But you won't like it," Charon told me.

"I don't think I could stand not knowing," I replied, all the while praying that it was not Jenny.

"His name is Nathan. He's Jenny's husband." My mind reeled, at first convinced it was a lie, or at least a mistake. The more I thought about it, however, the more plausible it seemed. I could only visit on weekends, Jenny would never answer her phone on weekdays, we either stayed indoors or went a few towns over for dates, and that tan mark! That damn white line around her ring finger; the most obvious clue in the world, and I'd never paid it much attention.

"What happens now?" I asked, feeling a bubbling rage rising within me.

"You go on to Hades. Nathan will get there in a few years, and then you can do what you like with him."

"And Jenny?"

"She won't be too far behind."

"Good," I nodded, accepting my fate. I shook the hand of the Ferryman and began my final walk into the storm.

Red Cape Publishing

HOME

And Other Stories

Collection VI

P.J. BLAKEY-NOVIS

# Quake

At school, I distinctly remember being taught the Earth sciences. My interest in these things only grew stronger into adulthood. I genuinely found it fascinating, impressive even. Volcanoes, earthquakes, tsunamis, and tornadoes, all with their immense power and potential to cause catastrophes on an unthinkable scale. I missed the opportunity to go to a regular university as I had already left home and needed to be working in order to support myself, but once I reached my early twenties, I decided to take up studying again, part-time. I completed a degree in Earth Sciences, which I passed with a decent grade, and naively thought I'd be able to walk into a position that I had always dreamed of. For the first six months I couldn't even find a relevant job to apply for. When I eventually did find something which sounded ideal, I could not get past the first stage of the interview due to lack of experience. Stupid bloody Catch-22; need the job to gain experience, need experience to get the job. And from then on, for the last fifteen years,

231

experiencing a natural disaster personally has only been a dream.

A lot of people would say that it is a strange dream to have, to want to be caught up in that kind of tragedy, and it is hard for me to explain the desire. I suppose it's similar to those guys who chase tornadoes across America, getting as close as possible to them, risking their lives for that adrenalin rush. I never thought I'd have the chance to realise this dream, living in the UK where disasters on this scale simply didn't happen, and not having the resources to travel anywhere that they did occur. The closest I had got to experiencing an earthquake at that time was at The Natural History Museum in London, where they have an 'earthquake room' which is supposed to simulate the 7.2 magnitude earthquake which hit Kobe in the winter of 1995. This all changed six months ago.

I'd never had much in the way of family. There were a number of people who I knew were related to me, but I had left my hometown at a young age and had very little contact with any of them. Even at Christmas, I only received perhaps two or three cards from family members, and I certainly never visited any of them. Which is why a letter from an aunt came as a

232

surprise. The name, Martha, only rang a vague bell in my mind and I could not recall ever seeing this person, or what she looked like. The letter explained that she had contacted my mother to request my address, and that her sister, another of my aunts, had passed away. I had no real feeling about this, as I did not know the woman. However, the now deceased Aunt Beryl had apparently been rather fond of me.

I don't know how Beryl's will had been split among the family, and what percentage my inheritance made up, but £15000 was a very welcome surprise. I contacted Aunt Martha by telephone, trying to sound saddened by the news of Beryl's passing, talked a little about myself and what I'd been doing for the last twenty or so years since we had seen one another. Martha told me that she had not wanted to send a cheque, in case it was lost in the post, so took my bank details in order to make a transfer. The money was in my account within two hours of ending our conversation.

The rest of the day passed in a blur of research and planning. I was well aware that most earthquakes occur around what has been dubbed *The Ring of Fire*, incorporating New Zealand, The

Philippines, Japan, and the western coasts of North and South America. My first thought had been to travel to Japan, but the visa would be restrictive and there was no guarantee I would experience an earthquake in the thirty days I was permitted to stay. It was as I looked into travelling to the Philippines that I came across the perfect solution - charity work. The company would arrange the visas, provide food and accommodation, and collect me from the airport. I only needed to make my way to Manila International Airport and make a charitable donation of £2000, then I could stay on for as long as I wished.

*** 

I took to the change well; I enjoyed the company of the other charity workers, loved working outdoors in the warmth, and took pride in the help we were providing for the local people. Over the first three months we experienced six minor earthquakes. They all scored low on the Richter Scale, and did very little damage, but the thrill was incredible. As soon as the first tremor could be felt, a rush of adrenalin hit me and I hoped, more than anything, that this would be a big one. There were no large earthquakes in the Philippines for the first five months of my visit but then it came. Although I felt the tremors, the epicentre was almost 100 miles away. We had no television in the camp, relying on the radio for news. The quake had not been as severe as the one in Kobe in 1995 but was not far off. The news reports described the carnage left behind, the death toll steadily rising into the thousands. This was what I had been waiting for, and I knew I could not keep away. Under the guise of wanting to see if I could help, I arranged transport to the site of the most destruction and was there less than twenty-four hours after the earthquake had struck.

Two of the other men from camp had offered to join me, and despite wanting to travel alone, I could think of no justification for turning down their help. The closest the rickety old bus could take us was a little over a mile from where the real damage had occurred, so the three of us made the rest of the journey on foot. Twenty minutes of walking, and we could smell the death in the air; that distinctive, metallic odour of spilled blood, a grim hint of flesh already beginning to decompose in the heat, and a sickening, burned smell. The emergency services were on the scene, gathered around fallen buildings, rescue dogs barking into dark corners of the destruction to announce the site of someone trapped.

My two associates from camp had already joined the team of rescuers in pulling at broken bricks and bent steel cables, desperate to get to the faint sound of the sobbing which came from within. I took the opportunity to slip away unnoticed, keen to explore the area of ground which had opened up so violently. There was an unmissable increase in the level of damage as I made my way towards the centre of what had been the town. I could see no buildings which remained intact, not even the Catholic church had survived this act of God. The whole scene appeared post-apocalyptic; as though humanity was on the verge of extinction, as if the entire globe now looked this way.

The streets were littered with rubble, and I had to take care as I made my way across the debris. At one point, I looked away from the ground and my foot made contact with something soft, in contrast to the bricks I had been walking across. I heard a wet sound and looked down, only to find I had trodden on what appeared to be the front half of a dog. I felt nothing for that poor creature, only a pull to find the place where the ground had opened; it was as though I was being called to it.

It had taken me thirty minutes to find my way to the edge of what was now a large crevice in the ground. I had counted no less than twenty-four dead bodies on my journey. At least, I presumed them to be dead judging by the amount of blood and impossible positioning of the limbs. I did not take the time to check them, and that makes me sound like a monster. The opening in the ground was not wide, less than a couple of feet, but its length seemed to continue for as far as I could see. The few rescue workers dotted about were too preoccupied with the injured to pay any attention to this strange westerner who was staring into the abyss.

There was no way of seeing how deep the crack was, but everything that I had studied suggested that earthquake cracks, even ones of this magnitude, were rarely more than a few feet deep. The way I saw it, that would be shallow enough to easily pull myself out of again, but I had to feel what it was like to be in there. Nervously, I glanced around to check that I wasn't being watched. Everyone was still absorbed in the rescue efforts, so I moved myself into a sitting position, legs hanging into the opening. As subtly as I could manage, I lowered myself in, my feet feeling their way down the muddy interior until they found an area solid enough to stand on.

I was in the hole up to my shoulders, so even at this end of the crevice the depth must have been around five feet. I suddenly realised how ridiculous I must look to those on the surface, just a head visible above the ground, and instinctively ducked out of sight. Although I had never read this as being fact, it seemed logical to me that the crack would get deeper towards the middle, before shallowing out again towards the other end. I did not know how long the crack went on for, but finding myself inside of it was exhilarating, and I shuffled myself along further.

There was an increase in depth, but only another couple of feet. I found myself enclosed, entombed perhaps, between two seven-foot walls of earth, but I was not afraid. I knew I could go back to where I had entered the ground and would be able to pull myself out. I have no way of knowing how long I was down there, but I recall making the decision to return to where I had started. That is when the second quake hit.

***

I can remember the tremors as the earth beneath my feet shifted, the sudden darkness as the loose ground above tumbled viciously on to me, and then only blackness. In hindsight, I should have expected it; most large earthquakes are followed soon after by a series of smaller ones, but the thought had never entered my head. When I came to, I found myself in total darkness, but able to move. My head hurt, as though it had been struck by something heavy, but the rest of my body seemed surprisingly unscathed. Moving my head in all directions, I could not find a single point at which light was able to penetrate the darkness and panic began to set it.

I knew I could not be far beneath the surface and reached up with the idiotic hope that I could simply push the overlaying earth away and call for help. Nothing budged, even a tiny amount, and my efforts only led to me getting a mouthful of damp mud as the loose soil tumbled down on to my face. I had no torch, of course, and no phone to use as a flashlight. I pressed the button on the side of my watch, hoping its meagre illumination would be of some assistance, but it did not respond. I ran my hand over its face and felt the crack in it, confirmation that the watch had not survived.

Sound does not travel well through the earth so, when the singing began, I thought someone on the surface had managed to create an opening. The sound became louder, a beautifully haunting sound which brought images of sailors and mermaids to my mind, but still no hint of light came with it. I sat there for an immeasurable amount of time, listening to what were unmistakably songs of some kind, strangely content at that moment. The trauma of my situation, the music, or quite probably both, sent me into a deep, yet fitful, sleep.

*** 

There was no alteration in the impenetrable darkness when I finally awoke, yet I knew that I was somewhere else. The air smelled different, cleaner perhaps. The singing persisted but more quietly; not further away, just not as loud as it had first been. The total lack of light, and therefore complete redundancy of my eyes, had heightened my other senses - in particular, my hearing. Now, the singing was not the only sound I could make out, but other noises alongside it. Scurrying, scraping, scratching.

"Who's there?" I called out in barely more than a whisper. My throat felt dry from a lack of water, and I had not uttered a word for what I presumed was many hours. There came no reply, but I knew I was not alone in these depths beneath the surface. I reached out my arms as far as they would go from my sitting position and felt nothing. I managed to pull myself to my feet, standing slowly for fear of hitting my head again. I reached full height without striking the earth above me. I reached my arms up, tip-toeing, and could feel nothing. Wherever I now was, it was much larger than when I had fallen asleep.

"Who's singing?" I asked. Still no reply. Beginning to get frustrated with the lack of response, and with a more rational fear setting in, I started to scream for help. Looking back, this should have been my very first response; at least then I knew I was close to the surface. Now, in this place, it felt deeper...much deeper. I managed to release the word *help* four times before something struck me in the chest, knocking me to the floor. The singing had stopped, and I found myself lying on my back with a weight on top of me.

Frozen, in both fear and surprise, I remained still and waited. My head involuntarily twitched to the side as I felt something graze my right ear. *A worm,* I thought. It had certainly felt like a worm, cold and slimy to the touch, but as more and more of these 'worms' touched the side of my face I knew they must be something else. I could feel them tracing lines down my cheeks, parallel with one another, five lines on each side. *Not worms, fingers!* I realised, pulling myself back as far as I could manage.

I was still being straddled by the owner of these worm-like appendages, and so I placed a hand on either side of the creature's waist and pushed it to one side. I managed to pull myself up to a standing position, heart racing, sweat pouring from my brow. I could see nothing but could sense movement in front of me. I wanted to scream for help, but that had angered my attacker before, and I was too terrified to do anything other than wait.

I felt the slimy parts touching my hands, feeling strangely like hands themselves; almost human in size but with unmistakable webbing between the fingers. I could feel the creature's breath on my throat, suggesting it was a few inches shorter than me. More than

242

anything, at that moment, I wanted to be able to see - to see what stood before me, to try to work out where I was, to find a way to escape. My curiosity, my obsession, had led me to this place and there was little doubt that this would become my grave.

The webbed hands ran all over my body as I stood completely still. When the inspection was complete, I heard damp footsteps as the creature moved away and resumed the singing. A dizziness came over me at the sound and I sat, soon falling again into a deep sleep.

***

When I awoke, the light hurt my eyes to the point that I could not fully open them for several minutes. It was a shock to the system, following the intense darkness I had found myself in and, when I did manage to focus on my surroundings, I knew I was no longer with the earth. The light filled the room, emanating from electric strip lights, made all the more intense by the clinical white of the room I found myself in.

I was in a bed, buried beneath a thick white duvet. In fact, everything in the room was white. I ached all over but could not be seriously injured as there were no tubes attached to my body, no machines beeping gently beside me, only silence. I cautiously lifted the covers to find that I was wearing a standard issue hospital gown. It was impossible to say how long I had been there, but I could not recall anything following my inspection by that vile creature. I hoped that I had merely slept for a matter of hours, but I was soon to learn that was far from the truth.

Sitting upright caused a wave of nausea to hit me, along with a dizziness that almost brought me tumbling from the side of the bed. I held the position, somewhere between horizontal and vertical, until the feeling passed enough for me to swing my legs toward the cold floor. There was too little sensation in my feet, a strange mix of pins and needles and numbness, and as I edged off the bed my legs gave way. I managed to place my hands out in front of me to break the fall a little, but my knees took a hard knock and I felt a strange, wet sensation in my abdomen.

Rolling myself over, I swung my almost useless legs out in front of me and used my hands to pull myself back so that I was able to rest against the spotless wall. The brilliantly white gown now showed a spreading crimson stain, and, in a panic, I lifted my gown to inspect the area. An inch or so beneath my navel was a line of stitches around six inches across. My movements had caused it to split at one end, and the blood now flowed freely. I watched in horror as the red liquid ran down between my legs and began to form a pool on the floor.

Frantically, my eyes darted around the room in search of a button to press which would summon the medical staff. I could find no button, no way of contacting anyone, so used my arms to crawl across the floor to the only door in the room, a trail of blood marking my path. I reached the door, but it took all my strength to pull myself up by the handle, only to find it locked. I bashed my fists against it until my hands were red, but no one came to my aid, and I could hear no sounds from beyond the locked door. The blood loss, combined with the exertion, caused me to lose consciousness, slumped against the door.

I was brought around by the door being pushed against me. I let out a quiet 'help', trying to roll myself away far enough for the door to be opened, far enough for someone to gain access and do something about this seemingly infinite supply of blood I was losing. My head felt light, and I had no doubt that I was close to bleeding out. I managed to keep my eyes open just enough to see the two figures enter the room. I had expected to see doctors' scrubs, or nurses' uniforms, so was shocked at the sight of two bright yellow haz-mat suits.

"What's going on?" I mumbled.

"Help me get him back onto the bed," I heard one of the men say. "Then find the bloody doctor. We need him alive." I let out a yelp as they lifted me, the wound in my abdomen tearing open further. I soon heard footsteps running along the corridor outside and the man who had helped me onto the bed appeared alongside a woman, holding a clipboard. I could just about make out her face through the protective suit; pretty, maybe mid-thirties, petite. I listened as the men explained they had found me slumped against the door. They pointed out the obvious trail of blood and the doctor nodded before sending the men on their way.

"What's going on?" I asked again, my hands instinctively pressed against the opening in my guts.

"You were found at the site of the earthquake," she replied in broken English. "That was almost six months ago." My head spun with shock. I hadn't been sleeping... I'd been in a coma.

"But, this wound," I said, raising my hands a little from the area. "This wound is recent."

"We had to perform a small procedure," the doctor continued. "We had to remove something." Now she had my full attention, even in my weakened state.

"Remove what?" I asked, my voice trembling. "Like a kidney? Or my appendix? And what's with the suits?" The doctor opened one of the drawers to my left, producing a vial and a worryingly long needed.

"We need to get you fixed up. This will help with the pain, and I will get those stitches repaired. Then we will be able to tell you everything, when you are well." Before I could protest, the needle found its way into my arm, the icy sensation of the morphine flowing through my veins rendering me unconscious in seconds.

*** 

I awoke in a panic, my first thought that months had yet again passed me by. This time, thankfully, the doctor was in the room when I came to.

"How long was I out?" I asked.

"Only a few days. We have you all fixed

up, but you really must stay in bed until you have healed." I thought back to our previous conversation, what I could recall of it.

"You said you had to remove something from me?" The doctor sat on the edge of the bed with a sigh.

"You were infected with something when you were found. At first, we were treating you for a head injury, and severe dehydration. You went through some scans and we found... an anomaly." She paused, and I could sense that she didn't want to be the one to break the news but continued regardless. "Something was growing within you."

"Like a tumour?" I asked, almost hopefully. A tumour wouldn't justify the suits, and the doctor's face gave away that it was something far worse.

"The procedure that you underwent was similar to a Caesarean section." She let that hang in the air for a moment. "Whatever *thing* you had encountered had placed something within you. We removed it, and it is being studied." Since I had awoken from the coma, I had been fixated on getting out of bed, working out why I was there. I had hardly given any thought to the earthquake but now it hit me like a slap in the face. That *thing,* the singing,

248

the webbed hands, the darkness.

"When can I leave?" I asked, not wanting to know any more about the surgery.

"That isn't my decision, I'm afraid. This is a military laboratory and you were found to be carrying life, the sort of which we have not seen before. For the time being, the government owns you." The doctor gave me a look filled with sadness, before turning to leave and locking the door behind her. I knew then that regardless what happens with the creature they had removed from me I wouldn't be leaving that facility again.

# Cemetery of the Living

I bury the dead in a cemetery. Nothing unusual there. Although the cemetery is one of my own construction and my definition of dead isn't quite the same as everyone else's. I've lost people who had, at some point, meant something to me. Through a series of betrayals, rejections, or simply growing apart, our relationships have died. Dead to me. No longer part of my life. And the dead deserve to be buried. My therapist said that grieving the loss of someone is an essential part of the healing process. Of course, she doesn't know I have three people buried on my land and I'm sure she'd be surprised to know they were buried a while before they really died.

When I was eighteen my girlfriend slept with my best friend. Naturally, I lost my temper, ended things, cut him off completely. Then I made the mistake of taking her back, only for her to do it again a year later. The second time hurt even more, knowing she'd never really been sorry, that it had all been an act. I hit her on the back of the head, she fell forward, cracking a temple on the corner of the coffee table. I was certain I'd killed her and, in an understandable state of panic (but not remorse, I realised), I headed outside.

My garden is larger than my house, which is not something I would have chosen really, but I'd inherited it at seventeen and couldn't wait to move into my own place. Now, it's not as if I'm in the middle of nowhere, but high fences and a few feet gap between houses mean I get enough privacy. No one saw me digging about in the garden during the early hours. On auto pilot, I excavated a trench, returned to the living room, only to find it corpse-less. The spots of blood from her gaping head wound led me to the bathroom where I found my girlfriend staring into the mirror in shock. I recall the dilemma clearly, the choices that came to mind. Apologise and hope for the best. Or don't. My body acted before my mind could rationalise, perhaps some primitive self-preservation instinct overriding morality. I hit her again, twice more, in fact, and she slumped to the linoleum floor. Without hesitation I picked her small frame up and slung her over my shoulder, headed though the door at the rear of my kitchen and launched her into the grave. I spent the night sitting in the dirt beside her, unable to bring myself to bury her, a plan forming in my head.

As daylight began to break, the woman I thought was the love of my life began to stir. Thankfully too weak to muster a scream, she could only murmur sounds of pain and confusion. I reached into the pit, sodden earth covering us both, and pulled her out. Even through her fear I could tell she was thankful to be out of the hole. Until I restrained her. After rummaging around in the garage I'd found a roll of duct tape and some cable ties - enough to keep her in place while I went hunting for supplies, once I'd cleaned myself up, of course.

As I climbed into my beat-up van I felt more alive than I ever had before. I had a plan, one I was sure would work. The sense of excitement from not only doing something illegal but the power that came with it was intoxicating. At that time, I didn't know how long I'd be able to keep her alive for. I had, however, expected her to make it for longer than she did.

The rest of that day feels like a blur, running on automatic to the shops, working in the garage (door closed), building a coffin, adding the airways, including a feeding hatch, sound-proofing the box.

At regular intervals I'd pop upstairs to check on my love and find she'd hardly moved, unable to even wriggle herself off the bed. Satisfied she wouldn't be going anywhere, I went through the usual routine of dinner and some television as I waited for night to fall.

When the darkness had become thick enough to cover my actions, I lugged the coffin from the garage to the garden, finding it a few inches too long for the pit I had dug. Another thirty minutes passed as I resized the hole in the earth and got her new home in place.

I returned to the bedroom, a knife in hand. A watched her eyes widen in fear but I had no intention of cutting her, the knife was for the cable ties and a little dramatic effect. I released her ankles, allowing her to walk, but kept her wrists in place. She didn't struggle against my touch until she saw the box. As she tried to turn on her heels I put the knife to her abdomen, quickly settling her down. I told her to get in, but she shook her head, tears falling. I shrugged before pushing her. She fell awkwardly, hitting her side hard on the coffin's edge as she landed. Again, as a way to induce fear more than any real threat, I slowly moved the blade towards her. I knew I needed to be quick. There would be a window of opportunity for her to make a move in between me removing her binds and closing the lid. She'd have the chance to try climbing out or, even worse, she could scream. I knew she'd force me to use the knife if she'd screamed and it wasn't what I wanted. I never wanted this experience to end.

Leaning over her, I snipped the cable tie as I yanked the tape away from her mouth. I heard her suck in a huge breath and I slammed the lid down before she could make another sound. The soundproofing was doing its job - I heard very faint sounds (largely coming through the air pipe) but knew they wouldn't travel far.

I whispered into the pipe, setting some rules. I told her to remain quiet, that if she couldn't then I'd have to take away her air supply. I explained I'd be back with food and water. That I'd look after her. I covered the coffin with some large boards I'd purchased and placed my garden bench on top. Nobody ever came to visit so there would be no one to question to change and the thin pipe protruding beneath the bench was barely noticeable.

She lasted almost a week. I can't say what the actual cause of death was, but the head wound had become infected and she had been lying in piss and shit from the second day onwards. It wasn't malnutrition though, I visited nightly, opening the hatch and delivering protein shakes and water. Her death hit me hard and it was a sad day when I filled the hole in fully and muttered my goodbyes.

As I mentioned earlier, there have been three. While my first may have been something which I made up as I went along, the others were undeniably premeditated. I honed my craft, improved on the design of the boxes, extended the lives of my next two conquests. My supposed friend, the one who my girlfriend had betrayed me with that first time, survived almost two weeks in the box. The third, a colleague who'd claimed my work as his own the previous year, lasted over a month, but I put this down to his larger frame. Through it all, beginning with the pain my lover inflicted on me, I consider myself having been reborn. I still attend therapy, god knows how I'd be without that, but I now know my purpose, the way to feel satisfied in the seeming pointlessness of life. I like to think my projects keep me sane, although I'm sure some people would disagree. It's been almost a year since I lost my last 'guest' but the next coffin awaits. It'll be filled soon, and I know it won't be the last.

# Deep Breaths

"Cause of death?" DC Matthews asked the coroner, her raspy, smoker's voice barely above a whisper.

"Her lungs both have a massive bloody hole in," he replied, dryly. "But that does seem to be the cause of death; there was minimal damage elsewhere on the body." Matthews glanced across the naked form in front of her as it lay on the metal gurney. The coroner's investigation had left marks of its own, of course, but the DC focused on those which had been inflicted in the last few hours of the young woman's life.

"Run me through what you've found," she ordered, her eyes still fixed on the thin lines of bruising around the girl's ankles.

"Well," the coroner began, clearing his throat. "As you can see, the victim has bruising around her wrists and ankles, presumably from being bound. We found small traces of fibre embedded in these places, which look to have come from a thin rope. There are a few fist-sized bruises to her lower back, but these are older. I'd say she already had these before the night she died. I found a small needle mark on her neck, just below her right ear. Toxicology is pointing to Flunitrazepam."

"That's Rohypnol?" The DC asked, despite being sure of the answer. The coroner nodded, pointing to the spot where an almost indiscernible puncture was present. "The nose is a weird one," he continued. Matthews had already noticed the odd shape of the dead woman's nose, how it appeared to be squashed, sucked-in on one side. There was a pause as Matthews waited for the coroner to elaborate.

"When she came in, both nostrils were closed. The left one is only open now because I opened it up. Her nose had been glued shut." The coroner looked at the DC, waiting for her to respond. Something akin to shock registered in her eyes for just a moment, but she kept her composure.

"With what? Superglue?" Matthews asked.

"Not the stuff you usually get in the shops. This looks more like surgical glue."

"So, it was from where? A hospital? Is that something that could be stolen by anyone, or am I looking at a medical professional for this?"

"A sample has gone to the lab. There are loads of brands, and they might be able to get a match. The public wouldn't have access to it from a hospital, but you can get it online easily enough." This wasn't what Matthews wanted to hear. "And finally, her lungs." The coroner led the DC over to the stainless-steel worktop where he had laid out various organs. Matthews had seen enough body parts to know what the lungs looked like, and it did not take a professional to see what was wrong with this pair. They both appeared equally deformed, contorted into a larger, anatomically impossible shape.

"This will make it clearer," the coroner explained, reaching for a bottle of distilled water and spraying it across the organs. As the water aided the removal of the drying blood, large tears could be seen in the lung tissue.

"And what would cause that?" Matthews asked, almost dreading the answer.

"Too much air," the coroner replied, simply. "There were no traces of any toxic substances in the lungs, so there is no reason to believe she had breathed in anything but normal air. Of course, she breathed in too much."

"So, she was injected with Rohypnol to knock her out, tied up, nose is glued shut, and what? Her lungs are pumped with air until they burst?"

"That's what it looks like," the coroner

258

shrugged. "As fucked up as that sounds, I don't see evidence of anything else. Just the bruises on her back, but they are older. I haven't noticed any similar cases to this. Have you?"

"I don't think so," Matthews replied, her mind racing as she attempted to put the pieces together. The methodology of this murder was new territory and seemed too extravagant to be a one-off.

\*\*\*

Marcus wanted to be famous, and the voice told him that he would be. At times he may have doubted his own sanity, but he never thought the voice could just be a part of his damaged mind. It sounded real, felt real. He could trace the presence of the voice, that terrible, demanding yell, back to when he was fifteen. Back, in fact, to a specific day: August 3rd, 2009.

He had spent the afternoon messing about in the woods with his friend Tom, smoking weed and drinking cheap vodka they had stolen from a supermarket. That was the day things had changed. The boys had been sat on a muddy slope, deep within the trees, chatting about girls. Marcus saw a squirrel on a branch across from them and, without thinking, picked up a piece of flint from the ground and launched it. He missed, and the squirrel disappeared into the thick leaves of the ash tree. But the voice came then, clear as anything he had heard, and he knew what he needed to do. As though possessed, he leapt up from the ground, grabbing broken branches and stones, hurling them all towards the spot he had last seen the squirrel. Nothing came of it, the poor critter presumably long gone by that point.

"What the fuck are you doing?" Tom screamed, pulling himself to his feet.

"It's just a squirrel," Marcus replied, eyes still searching for a glimpse of the grey fur.

"I know, but you're going a bit crazy there. Maybe take it easy of the weed?" Marcus looked at his friend, his only real friend, with a look of pure disgust. Tom noticed the flicker of rage in Marcus's eyes and took a step back. "Let's go back to mine," Tom suggested, no longer feeling safe in the woods.

"You ever get the urge to kill something?" Marcus asked, a slight grin appearing on his face. Tom took another step back.

"Nope," he replied honestly. "I want to go home now."

"I want to go home now," Marcus

mimicked, stepping towards his friend. "So, go, no one is stopping you."

"Are you coming?" Tom asked as he retreated further.

"Not yet. I'll call you later." Tom did not reply, simply turning on his heels and making his way out of the forest as quickly as he could. Marcus chose to stay well into the night, searching for a creature he could drain the life from, but failed to find anything larger than an insect.

\*\*\*

Eight years on, and he hadn't spoken to Tom for two years. He had hardly spoken to anyone, in fact, aside from the voice which gave him his orders. Stomping on insects had progressed to killing small animals which he would buy from pet shops. The methods had altered over time - the initial rush he felt from simply dropping a rock on a guinea pigs head soon became insufficient, and Marcus performed gruesome experiments on the creatures that were unfortunate enough to fall into his hands. Over the years he had killed hundreds of animals, mostly small, occasionally as large as cats and dogs. He slit a cow's throat one time but almost got caught as he headed home in blood-soaked clothing. It was inevitable that he would move on to people before too long.

The voice had become more persistent, more controlling. Who, or what, it belonged to needed blood, fed on agony and suffering. It compelled Marcus to watch the most disturbing videos he could find online, to read the most graphic stories. Marcus became obsessed with serial killers and their methods, as well as their legacies. He read countless books about murderers, studied medical journals looking for inspiration as to how to inflict wounds that would not cause immediate death, and felt his interest pulled towards the occult.

In 2017, Marcus discovered that he did not merely need to listen to the voice; he could converse with it. They shared conversations within Marcus's mind for hours on end, about many different subjects. But no matter what the topic was, it always came back to one thing - murder. The voice told Marcus that he was a vessel, a host, and that he would be carrying out great work. *There is no appreciation of life, without death,* it would tell him. *Make them afraid, make them determined to live their best lives while they still have the chance. Let them know that death is coming for them.*

"What are you?" Marcus had asked, on numerous occasions. The question was largely ignored or answered vaguely until the owner of the voice decided to give more information. *I am elemental, a part of the Earth, as I am part of the universe, and all that exists beyond it. I am the opposite of life; death, if you like. This does not mean I am anti-life; far from it. Life for you humans varies so much in quality that it seems unfair. Children die in their thousands from lack of food and clean water, yet so many others eat until they are full and produce so much waste. Parents feed their children from food banks just so they can keep a roof over their heads, while other kids get every new piece of mind-numbing technology. The only thing that is fair, that is guaranteed regardless of circumstances, is that death will come. My purpose, if I could be said to have one, is to make people appreciate what they have, no matter how much that may be. And that's where you come in.*

Marcus understood the general idea the voice was trying to convey - people needed to fear death in order to appreciate life. The elemental part stayed at the forefront of his thoughts as he considered his first kill. Elemental. Elements. Four elements.

"Who deserves to be first?" he asked,

eyes transfixed on a video he had found about autopsies. *It doesn't matter who dies. The point is that it should be random. Male, female, young, or old. So long as the gesture is grand enough to make the masses tremble.*

\*\*\*

In September 2017, Marcus called Tom. They had exchanged a few messages over the years, met up a few times when they happened to be near one another (Tom having moved away at 18). They had never spoken about that afternoon in the woods, but it had fractured their friendship instantaneously.

"You about at the weekend?" Marcus asked casually.

"Not down your way, but I'm not busy," he replied. "Why, what's up?"

"Thought I'd come and visit," Marcus suggested. "I haven't been to yours yet and you've been there years!" There was a pause on the line.

"Six years, yeah. And you haven't wanted to come here until now. What's going on?"

"I felt bad that we didn't get to hang out much, and I'm bored in this fucking town all the time. Thought it'd be fun. You got space for me to stay?" Tom took a moment to think it over.

"Yeah I do. I could do with the company, to be honest," he said, starting to open up. "Marie left me. I'll tell you about it when you get here. Want me to pick you up from the station?" he asked.

"That'd be great," Marcus replied. "Beers and a takeaway Friday?"

"Wouldn't you rather go out for drinks?" Tom asked, having assumed they would be heading to the pub for a session.

"I didn't know if you felt up to it? You sound a bit down. Be easier to chat and catch up if we stay in. Maybe go out Saturday?" Marcus suggested, not wanting to be seen in public with Tom any more than necessary. Tom, on the other hand, wasn't sure he even wanted to hang out with Marcus at all, especially not just the two of them in his flat but decided to see how the evening went.

By eight o' clock on the Friday, Marcus and Tom were a few beers down and plating up a curry which had been delivered. Tom had put on some music, and the two men spent the evening catching up. Tom did almost all the talking, mostly about Marie, and Marcus nodded in the right places. Tom was clearly heartbroken, unable to understand why his four-year relationship had ended so abruptly.

"I thought we were fine," he explained. "Things had got a bit stale, I guess, but she seemed happy enough. I just need to know why she left." Marcus watched as Tom tried to stop himself from crying.

*She met someone else,* the voice in Marcus's head announced. It seemed so loud that Marcus jumped, certain that Tom must have heard it too. "How do you know?" Marcus whispered, catching Tom off-guard.

"How do I know what?" he asked, puzzled.

"How do you know she was happy?" Marcus replied quickly, trying to back-pedal. "You don't think there was someone else?"

"I have no idea, but I had no reason to think there was. She won't reply to my messages or calls; it's as if she's completely forgotten me."

"But you have other friends, right? People you can hang out with, people to check in on you?" Marcus asked, not out of concern for his friend.

"Not really," Tom replied. "Sometimes I go out with the guys from work on a Friday, but all I had was my job, and

Marie." *Do it now,* the voice demanded. *Make it quick, and you can be on a train home tonight!* The pair sat in silence for a few moments before Tom announced that he needed the bathroom. Four elements. Water. Air. Earth. Fire. The bathroom has plenty of water.

Marcus kept his position on the sofa until he heard the splash of urine hitting the water in the bowl. He had not heard the door click shut so, quickly and quietly, he made his way along the hallway. His plan of attack ran through his head as he approached Tom, a rush of adrenalin flowing through him. *Do it!* the voice seemed to scream in his head.

Before Tom could even zip up his trousers, Marcus landed two hard punches to his lower back, causing him to yelp in surprise as well as pain. Before he could fully turn around, Marcus grabbed hold of Tom's shirt, kicking his legs out from under him. There was a thud as Tom's head hit the edge of the bathtub on the way down. Dazed, and under the influence of the beers, he could do little to fight back. Marcus quickly thrust Tom's head into the toilet, his face just reaching the surface of watery piss. Marcus held him still as he brought the toilet lid down and sat upon it, his weight trapping Tom there.

Marcus flushed, as Tom kicked out his legs and arms, trying to free himself. Tom's face was not submerged enough to drown him, but the water from the flush caused him to splutter and take in mouthfuls of fluid. Marcus continued to press the flush, as soon as the cistern had filled. The constant flood of water into Tom's mouth, coupled with the pressure of the toilet seat against the back of his neck restricting his airways, meant that he was dead in six flushes. Marcus was overjoyed. *Perfect,* the voice praised. *Find his phone, delete the messages from you, and the call log.* Marcus did as he was told. He also deleted the number of the takeaway from the call log, in case the police learned that two meals had been delivered. Then he got the map up on his phone and took the twenty-minute walk back to the station, just in time for the last train home.

***

After Tom's murder, the voice had gone quiet. Marcus assumed that its desire had been sated, at least for the time being. The months following that Friday evening had been tense, as Marcus waiting for official news of Tom's death, or the dreaded arrival of the police. Nothing came. The murder made the front page of the local paper in Tom's hometown but was quickly forgotten, the police having had no leads, and was added to the list of unsolved crimes for that year.

Eighteen months passed before the voice made an appearance again. Marcus had been able to resist killing for the most part, having satisfied his urges with the occasional cat, but had not put any real thought into taking another human victim. The voice, however, was able to get him more in the mood for blood.

*It's time,* it stated, as though it were time to leave for work, or head to bed. Marcus nodded in understanding. Who should be next? And how? Marcus had no idea. He knew it needed to be random, so the method could be planned, as well as the venue, but the victim would just be whoever was in the wrong place at the wrong time. *Four elements,* came the voice. *Water. Air. Earth. Fire.*

"Water is done," Marcus muttered. "Air? How can you kill someone with air? You mean take the air away?" Marcus's mind wandered onto thoughts of placing a bag over his victim's head and securing it around the neck with duct tape. *Too much of a good thing can be bad for you,* the voice suggested, rather cryptically. "Too much air?" Marcus wondered. Then it all seemed so obvious.

There was no doubt that Marcus would need to take his victim from a public place; Tom had been the only person he knew well enough to be able to get into their home. He needed to be able to not only overpower them, but also to be able to move the body somewhere discreet. *It must be a woman,* the voice pointed out.

"Perhaps I could grab a jogger?" Marcus said aloud. *Perhaps you could,* the voice replied. *But, for what you have planned, smaller, less healthy lungs would be advisable.* "Not a child," Marcus stated. "I'm not ready for that." *I didn't say a child,* said the voice. *But do whatever you like, this is your show.*

\*\*\*

Marcus spent a few months deliberating over the details of his plan. Even after trying to consider every eventuality, it was far from fool-proof. Nevertheless, finding a small, female smoker, preferably drunk, and after dark, led him to one possible place - the only nightclub in town. It attracted a crowd of teenagers due to the slack checking of identification, and the vast majority of patrons were in the sixteen to nineteen age group, aside from a few dirty old men who went there to try their luck with the young women.

Marcus had never been inside the place but spent his Friday and Saturday evening watching the club empty out around 2am. He watched as drunken teenagers staggered into the street, shouting, puking, stumbling, and sometimes fighting. There were plenty of girls in the groups as they left, some latched on to whoever was taking them home that night, some in pairs having refused the advances of the men on the hunt. The plan had been merely to observe, but fate threw someone perfect his way.

Marcus had watched a pair of young women, around twenty years old, stagger down a side street with their arms linked. Keeping a safe distance, he followed behind, in case they separated somewhere along the way. Two roads on and they did just that, seeming to have reached the home of one of them. They hugged, and Marcus just about could make out their conversation from where he stood.

"You can stay here, you know?"

"It's fine, he'll go berserk if I'm out all night," the smaller woman replied.

"I don't know why you put up with it,"

she was told. "I mean, I understand him wanting to know you're safe, that's fair. But now you've let him get away with hitting you, he's going to do it again. You know that."

"If he does, then I'll leave him. I promise. I'll text you when I get home," and after a peck on the cheek, the girls parted company. Marcus continued his hunt, wondering how long it would be before they reached the woman's home, and if there was anywhere suitable on the way for him to carry out his plans. His backpack contained the necessary paraphernalia but finding a safe location could be difficult.

He followed towards the end of the lengthy road they were on, certain that the sound of his footsteps, even his breathing, would give him away before long. Just before the road came to an end, there was a gravel path to the right. Marcus knew it would be shrouded in total darkness at this time of night, and he was aware it may be his only opportunity. As quietly as he could manage, he slipped the bag from his back and slowly unzipped it. Taking out the hypodermic needle, Marcus held it poised, ready. He knew that the Rohypnol would usually take a good fifteen minutes to kick in, but the dose he held was enough to take down a large man in that time, so hoped the petite girl would succumb to its effects in a shorter time. *Only one way to find out,* the voice stated. The girl was a few metres away from the gravel path when Marcus seized his chance. He ran towards her, but in her drunken state she had only just begun to turn when he jabbed the syringe into her neck. Cupping a hand over her mouth to muffle her cries, Marcus dragged her into the darkness of the track.

***

There was a disappointment in having to rush, but it was too late to stop now. Fumbling in the dark, Marcus pulled out two lengths of rope to bind her wrists and ankles together. She had become drowsy in seconds, and it was unlikely that she would feel much of what was going to happen to her. *The ropes were probably unnecessary,* he thought, as she lay almost perfectly still in the dirt. Marcus retrieved the surgical glue from his bag, squirting a generous amount into each of his victim's nostrils before holding them shut. Still, she did not move, but her mouth had opened in response, trying to compensate for the lack of air entering via

273

her nose. Marcus held the position for a few minutes, listening out for any sign that he would be disturbed. Satisfied that he was safe for the time being, he lifted his hand away.

The girl's nose felt strange in the darkness, thin and compressed. The glue did its job, completely sealing off both nostrils. The time had come for the final act. Marcus took the foot-pump from his backpack, a cheap one designed for inflating airbeds and beach toys, and proceeded to force the attachment down the girls throat. There was no struggle, almost no movement, as the drug left her immobilized. Slowly, he began to pump.

The sound was deafening in the silence, and he was certain he would be caught at any moment. Panic caused him to pump harder, and for a while he was unsure if it was even working. He watched the girl's chest rise, almost imperceptibly at first, but then the shape of her seemed to change. She appeared bloated, her breasts pushing upwards. Then came the first pop. One lung had ripped open from the pressure, causing a rush of adrenalin within Marcus, pushing him to pump harder. The second lung went the same way after a few seconds, and it was done.

Aware of the risk involved in hanging

274

around, Marcus quickly removed the ropes and the pump, slung them into his bag, and crept away into the darkness.

*Water and Air complete,* the voice reminded him. *Fire and Earth are next.*

# Shielded

The caravan park took the brunt of the storm that day, a freak weather occurrence is what the news called it. Static homes overturned, cars dragged across gravel coated parking areas, bins launched into the air. Thirteen dead. Nothing outside the perimeter of the park was touched. Matthew was five that day and right in the middle of it. Literally, dead centre, yet untouched. Experts put it down to the boy being in the eye of the storm but were unable to explain how he remained in there for the duration of the event. The protective sphere he'd thrown around himself had gone unnoticed.

Matthew did not speak for some time after the storm. He met the questions thrown at him by therapists, doctors, and the authorities with a distant stare. Nobody could get any response from him, so he was vaguely diagnosed with PTSD and largely left to the care of his single mother, Liz, who had watched through terror-filled eyes as the storm raged and her young boy sat in the middle of it, seemingly oblivious to the destruction. Her instinct had been to run from their static home and throw her arms around Matthew, but something held her back. The caravan shifted on its foundations, the sound of concrete scaping on metal only adding to the horrific howls of the wind. She stared at her only child, his hair not even lifting with the gale, and knew pulling him into the home would be far too dangerous.

Months of play therapy sessions at school were not enough to get the words from Matthew's mouth, but progress was made. Liz met with the therapist on a monthly basis and during the tenth meeting there was finally more to be said. Previous meeting had become predictable – still not speaking, plays with the paint and sand well, draws 'normal' pictures. This time, however, Matthew's artwork had taken a turn. The therapist held up a large sheet of paper covered in black crayon. Despite the boy's young age, there was no mistaking what the image depicted. Crudely drawn caravans covered the page at various angles, some completely overturned. At the centre was little more than a stickman drawing but surrounding the figure was a dome.

Liz explained that she saw no such thing on the day of the storm and the therapist agreed that it would be

277

impossible for it to be a literal dome. It surely had to be the way Matthew explains how he *felt* on that day, as though something sheltered him from the aggressive weather. If Matthew had been able to speak then he could have told them differently.

Liz was allowed to keep the illustration and showed it to Matthew that evening. He shrugged, as though the meaning were obvious. Still he did not speak. As the winter approached, the weather turned colder, the winds whipping at their home. In such an exposed location, this was something they had grown accustomed to, but since that awful day, each scream of wind against the windows brought a pang of anxiety. Liz did her best to hide her fears for the sake of her son. Matthew clung to her whenever the wind became noticeable, yet he did not seem afraid – if anything, he was acting in a protective manner.

December 9th began like any other day but both Matthew and Liz knew the significance. A candle-lit vigil had been planned for that evening to mark the first anniversary of the tragedy. Matthew scrawled on paper in badly spelled writing that they should go somewhere else that day. Liz shook her head sadly and explained there was nowhere else *to* go. She did her best to reassure him that all would be okay but struggled to believe her own words.

Fifty-eight people gathered near the centre of the caravan park that evening, candles in hands, mourning their loved ones. Matthew did not take his hand from his mother's, squeezing it even more tightly as the wind began to grow. It started with a gentle breeze but was quickly strong enough to snuff out the candles. The crowd exchanged nervous glances but hid their concerns as best they could. It took only minutes for the wind to be strong enough to shake trees and blow the caps from the some of the men. A woman screamed, sending a wave of panic through the group. Parents grabbed their children, the elderly fled on unsteady feet, all returning to the perceived safety of their static homes. Matthew watched as a young couple reached the door to their home, only to have an enormous oak tree crash through the caravan's roof. Coincidence? A freak storm hitting on the same date a year later in the exact same place had to mean something, even Matthew could see that.

Liz yanked Matthew's arm and pulled him towards their home, almost being knocked down by a metal dustbin the wind appeared to have launched at them deliberately. Matthew resisted, having seen the caravan move about last time. Something told him they would be no safer inside, but Liz insisted. The pair hunkered down beneath the small dining table, covering their ears, while Liz muttered desperate prayers to a God she had never believed in.

Above the raging howls of the wind came a sound like tearing metal – a vicious sound as though an enormous beast was chewing its way through to them. Liz felt the force of the wind before registering that the roof had been completely torn away. Mugs fell from the table, crashing down beside Matthew. Pictures began to drop from the walls, only to be whipped into the air and taken away forever. Liz clung to Matthew with all her might as furniture began to move. The table she had hoped would protect them began to rock. She watched in horror as it lifted a few inches from the ground, dropped back down, then rose again. It would soon be gone and then nothing could save them. Nothing but Matthew.

As the table disappeared through the gaping hole above them, stillness overwhelmed Liz. The sound of the wind, that unbearable, angry roar, stopped entirely. The force of the air pushing against them ceased in an instant. Looking around, everything was still being thrown about, the storm continued to rage, but all Liz could hear was the sound of her breathing. She looked at Matthew, her face a mixture of confusion, panic, and fear. He simply smiled back at her and squeezed her hand a little more tightly.

He knew this wouldn't be the last time the storm came for him, just as he knew it didn't matter where he tried to hide. He made himself a promise then, a promise he would keep his mother safe. The storm, whatever it really was, was after him. She would not be safe all the time he was with her but if he ran away he knew she would search for him. The protective sphere disappeared, the sudden cacophony causing Liz to cover her ears once more. Matthew stepped away from her and reinstated the shield. Liz could swear she heard him shout *'I love you Mummy'* as he was dragged through the opening and into the sky.

Liz screamed, trying to stand yet unable to leave the protective confines of the dome. Matthew flew above the caravan park, carried on the maleficent winds, spinning in all directions. He did not know where he was being taken and had no intention of finding out. With just a thought, he wrapped himself in a sphere and felt himself dropping to the ground, landing as though covered in bubble wrap. He looked towards his old home, thought of the grief his mother would feel for the rest of her life, and allowed a solitary tear to fall. *It's for the best,* he reminded himself, wondering how long he could really survive on his own.

# The Flames of Hell Are Coming

The flames had surrounded the only viable exit points by the time the smoke had pulled me from my slumber. My wife, Jessica, just beginning to rouse, spluttered wet coughs. Dark plumes of noxious smoke billowed from beneath the door, filling our bedroom, stinging eyes and throats. I knew not to grab at the metal doorknob, as it would certainly be too hot to touch, and I kicked at the door half-heartedly. The door refused to budge, and I knew we were finished. I could see in Jessica's eyes that she understood as well.

"The girls..." she murmured, fearful for the safety of our twelve-year-old twins. "You need to save them."

I smiled sadly. "No, I don't. This is for the best." I uttered the words too quietly for my wife to hear, knowing she wouldn't understand things the way I did. It was too late for any of us now.

*Yesterday*

"How have they been today?" I asked Jessica upon my return from work. I'd been on edge, worried about how well my wife was coping with the girls. They had been acting up for some months, in small ways, and I could see she was struggling with it.

"Bearable," she told me. "But only just. It has to be hormones, right? I mean, they are almost teenagers. I don't remember playing up like this when I was their age, though."

"I'm sure you were a force to be reckoned with," I said with a forced smile, kissing Jessica on the forehead. "I'm glad it hasn't been too bad."

"No, just the usual; winding each other up, slamming doors, ignoring me," she explained.

"Where are they now?"

"Playing upstairs. They kept on at me to let them go into the attic, so I gave in."

"We haven't even been up there yet," I replied, surprised that my wife would allow the girls up there without us checking that it's safe.

"I poked my head through the hatch. The lights work up there, and there are a few boxes which must have been left by the previous owners. It's all boarded on the floor, so they won't be falling through the ceiling."

I nodded, satisfied that my wife had taken reasonable precautions, before heading upstairs to take a look myself.

"Emily, Victoria," I called out from the hallway landing, gazing up through the hole in the ceiling above me. The wooden stairs which pull down for access were out, and I placed a foot on the first one. "Girls?" I called out again. *Ignoring me too, I guess.* I began to climb the stairs and, poking my head through the opening, found my daughters sitting on the wooden flooring opposite one another, legs crossed, flicking through what appeared to be an old photo album.

"What you got there?" I asked, pulling myself the rest of the way into the attic. Still, they seemed oblivious to my presence. "Hello?" I said, a little louder, and this finally got their attention.

"Jesus, Dad!" Emily said. "Don't sneak up on us like that!"

"I didn't," I said, a little surprised at the aggression in Emily's voice. "I was calling you. What you looking at?"

"What does it look like?" Victoria retorted in her now trademark sarcastic tone.

"It looks like a photo album," I replied, unable to hide my own sarcasm. "Where'd you get it?" Victoria simply rolled her eyes, a common response from her which I had learned to ignore.

"It was in this box," Emily told me, nodding towards a large cardboard box to her left. "There are loads of albums in there, and they look really old." I took a seat beside Emily and picked up the album. The cover simply stated *Christmas*. Flicking through, it showed pictures of a family enjoying a multitude of Christmases. The pictures weren't dated, but the two young boys in the photos took the same pose by the tree each year from the age of around two, to perhaps twelve or thirteen. Judging by the permed hair and prevalence of orange and browns, I'd guess at them having been taken, mostly, in the seventies.

"We looked through another one called *Holidays*," Emily told me, "but it was mostly pictures of these boys on a beach which I thought was pretty boring. Did they used to live here?"

"I guess so," I replied. "We bought the house from the Stevenson's, but this isn't them in the photographs. So, maybe it was the owners before that." All the while, Victoria still did not speak to me, or her sister for that matter, simply sitting in her position and staring at the box of photo albums.

"Dinner time!" was yelled up through the opening in the attic floor, Jessica's voice interrupting our investigation.

"Come on then girls, let's go eat."

"Can we come back up after dinner?" Emily asked me. She seemed to be thoroughly enjoying nosing through other people's things, and I had to admit I was enjoying the time with her. It was just a shame that Victoria was being so cold.

"What do you think, Victoria? Wanna come back up and see what treasure we can find after dinner?" I asked, trying to keep my tone as jolly as I could. All I got was a typical *'whatever'*, before Victoria started making her way down to the dining room. "I'll take that as a yes then," I mumbled.

Dinner passed in near silence with Emily only briefly telling her mother what they had found so far, and Victoria refusing to speak to anyone. After we had eaten, I tried to coax Jessica into joining us, hopeful that some 'family time' would be beneficial. Using the washing-up as an excuse, she declined.

Emily and I spent an hour or more flicking through the remaining albums in the box, watching that same family grow and experience a very ordinary life.

"Why do they stop here?" Emily asked me, having noticed that there were no more photographs of the boys any older than perhaps thirteen.

"I guess that's how old they were when they moved?" I suggested, unable to think of anything else to offer. "It's a bit odd that they have so many well-organised photo albums and that they left them behind, though."

"They didn't leave," Victoria said from the other side of the attic. I was certain that I must have misheard her, so I grunted a 'huh?' in her direction.

"They didn't leave," she repeated.

"What do you mean?" I asked. Emily looked anxious and I was about to lose my temper if Victoria was trying to scare her sister.

"What?" Victoria asked, seeming to notice me for the first time in a while.

"I said, what do you mean they didn't leave?"

"Who?"

"Oh, for God's sake Victoria. You just said the family in the photos didn't leave!" I said, a little louder than I had expected.

"Whatever," she replied, looking confused. Emily and I looked at each other with an equal measure of concern and bewilderment.

"Emily, are there any more albums?" I asked, trying to distract our thoughts from Victoria's strange outburst. She made her way around the attic, opening boxes and reporting her findings to me.

"There are a few stuffed toys, old cookbooks, Christmas decorations..." Emily paused to hold up a battered fairy that I recognised from the festive photographs, before slinging it back in the box. "That's about it. Have you found anything interesting, Vicky?" No reply.

"Victoria, if you don't sort out your attitude then you can go and sulk in your room. I'm getting sick of the silent treatment, no one is making you stay up here with us." I had raised my voice enough for Jessica to hear and she began calling up through the opening in the hatch.

"Everything okay up there?" Jessica asked, and I could hear the creak of the stairs as she took the first few, allowing her to poke her head through the opening.

"All fine," I replied. "Just getting a bit fed up with being ignored."

"Welcome to my world," she said with a knowing look. "Another half hour then the girls need to get ready for bed. School tomorrow." Jessica was gone before I could respond. Victoria was still rooting through a box in the corner of the attic; she had been going through it since we had returned from dinner. Asking what she had found was futile, so I decided to take a look for myself.

"Let's take a look at what you've found," I announced, approaching this near-teenage monster. Victoria was elbow-deep in a large box, various pieces of bric-a-brac lying on the ground around it, presumably pulled from the box so far. I placed a hand gently on her back as I came to a stop beside her and that's when she freaked out. There is no other way to describe it. Victoria slapped my hand away from her, frantically gathering all the items from around the box and placing them back inside before turning to face me.

"This box is mine," she said, her voice monotone, eyes flashing something akin to anger, something primal. Instinctively, I took a step back.

"Vicky," I began, concern flowing into my voice. "If you girls find anything you want up here then you're welcome to keep it. I can't imagine the owners will be wanting any of it."

"This box is mine," she repeated.

"Okay, well why don't we have a look through it together and see what you've found?" I suggested. I didn't especially care what junk the girls decided was worth holding on to, but if there was something worth having in that box then I didn't want Emily to miss out. I reached a hand towards the box. Emily had approached us, equally curious as to what lie within. My hand didn't make it far enough to make contact, as Victoria shoved me away from it. I lost my footing and landed on my backside, rage building inside me. Before I could shout at my daughter, she spoke.

"It's my fucking box! I fucking told you that. If you touch it, I'll end you." The words came out like a growl, deep and guttural, and for an instant I felt truly afraid of my own daughter. Emily began to cry, dashing for the stairs out of the attic and down to perceived safety. I could hear her yelling *'mum!'* over and over.

"Go to your room!" I screamed, unable to think of anything else to say that wouldn't make the situation worse. I needed her away from me so that we could both calm down. As soon as the words had left my mouth, I saw a glint of something in Victoria's eyes, a change. Once again, it was as though she had just recognised me. She appeared confused, not understanding why I had yelled at her, but stomped to her room and slammed the door anyway.

Jessica and I sent Emily to the living

room to watch television, while we went over the peculiar events in hushed tones in the kitchen. I explained everything, my wife's eyes widening when I repeated what Victoria had said, word for word. We decided to wait until the girls were definitely asleep, before checking out the contents of that box for ourselves.

Desperate for the girls to get to sleep, the evening dragged on painfully. Once we were satisfied that the coast was clear, Jessica and I made our way back up into the attic. I pointed out the box in the far corner, the one that Victoria had become obsessed with, and we approached it with some hesitation. *It's just a box of junk,* I told myself, trying to recall the items that Victoria had scattered about the floor. I could not remember what any of them were. Jessica placed her hands on the cardboard flaps, opening two at once. No sooner had she done so than the silence of the house was shattered by an awful scream. We looked at one another for the briefest moment before both turning to leave the attic.

The girls' rooms were next to one another, along the hallway from the attic entrance. There was no way to tell which twin had unleashed the terrifying sound, so we ran straight into one room each. I found myself in Emily's room, causing her to begin stirring in her sleep. Before I could back out of there, another scream filled the air. This time there was no mistaking that it came from Jessica. Within seconds I was standing behind my wife, a *what the fuck?* leaving my mouth, barely audibly.

Victoria was standing on her bed, a knife from the kitchen in her hand. She had been carving strange symbols into the wall, none of which I recognised. She seemed oblivious to our presence and Jessica went to approach our daughter. I placed a hand on her shoulder to keep her back.

"Vicky?" I said, staying at a distance. "What are you doing?" No reply. "I'm going to come over there, okay?" I'd be lying if I said I wasn't afraid, but I had little choice in the matter. I couldn't very well leave her to destroy the walls and there was no doubt that something was very wrong. I came alongside Victoria, watching as she continued to carve deep scratches into the newly painted wall above her bed. I reached for her, fearful of being pushed again, or worse. "Vicky?" I repeated, barely above a whisper. My hand made contact with her nightdress and she snapped, just as she had done earlier.

293

"Don't touch me, you fucking pervert!" she yelled, leaping from the bed, knife raised. She would most certainly have stabbed me right then if I had not been swift in grabbing her wrists. I twisted the one which held the knife, forcing her to drop it, before kicking her legs out from underneath her and dumping her on the bed. Jessica ran to retrieve the knife as I stood poised for another attack.

"Vicky," I said, waiting for a response, but she was already asleep. Jessica and I backed quietly out of the room, closing the door behind us. I poked my head into Emily's room to find she had remained asleep, thankfully, and we headed to the living room to process what had just happened.

"What did she mean?" Jessica asked me, her eyes watery, jaw set.

"When?"

"When she called you a fucking pervert?" There was no mistaking what was going through my own wife's mind at that moment and I felt sick.

"I have no idea!" I retorted, the shock evident. "What are you suggesting?" I returned her glare and she finally conceded.

"Nothing. But it's a weird thing to say."

"All of it was fucking weird!" I replied.

"The symbols, the swearing, the violence. I'm really worried."

"Do you think something has happened to her? You hear about this odd behaviour when children get... you know," Jessica let her voice trail off.

"I don't know," was all I could manage, unwilling to consider that someone may have hurt my baby. "And I don't know what we do now."

Jessica and I spent the remainder of the evening staring at the television, barely talking to one another. The events of the evening were weighing heavily on both our minds and neither of us suggested returning to the attic. It felt as though looking into that box of old junk would trigger some other disaster, and it wasn't a risk we were willing to take just yet. Sleep came hard for me and, when it eventually did, it was filled with the darkest of dreams.

I awoke from a nightmare a little after 6am and decided to get myself up before anyone else. I enjoyed a coffee in the peace of the early morning, feeling a little better about things in the light of day. This morning, when the girls had left for school, I would bring that bastard box out of the attic and get rid of the contents, regardless of what they were.

The silence of the morning was broken by the sound of cries coming from Victoria's bedroom and I rushed to her, almost spilling my coffee in my haste. My first thought was that I would be greeted by a repeat of last night's terror, so it was almost a relief to find Victoria crying in a 'normal' fashion. She was sat on the edge of her bed, gazing up at the strange carvings in the wall when I found her.

"Hey," I said, trying to keep the tone as cheery as possible. "How you feeling now?"

"I'm really sorry Dad," she said between sobs. "I can't believe I did all that!"

"Do you remember doing it?" I asked. I had half-expected her to be freaking out because of the mess in her room, with no recollection of how it had happened.

"Sort of," she tried to explain. "I mean, it feels like I did it in a dream, like I wasn't really in control of what I was doing." I was about to ask her if she felt well enough for school but stopped myself. Perhaps it was selfish of me, but I needed her out of the house while I disposed of that box.

"Well, you get yourself ready for school and I'll make you some breakfast. Don't worry about the mess; I'll clear it up while you're out." I heard a 'Thanks, Dad', as I made my way to the kitchen. The morning passed in the same way that hundreds had done so before, almost to the point where things felt completely normal. I called work and told them that I had an urgent family issue and needed to take the day off but would return tomorrow. Jessica did the same and, as soon as the girls were safely making their way down the road, I explained my plans.

"We need to get back up there," I said, pointing to the ceiling. Jessica nodded but could not make eye contact with me. She looked afraid but I did not know if she feared the box, Victoria, or me. "Don't worry," I told her. "I'll go and get it. I'll just tape the whole thing up and take it to the dump." Again, Jessica nodded, before taking her coffee to the living room and turning on the television. "And once I've done that, I'll pop to the hardware store for some filler and paint so we can get Vicky's room sorted before she gets home." There was no reply from Jessica, but I could imagine she was simply nodding again.

As much as I would strongly deny the presence of anything supernatural in the real world, it was impossible to ignore the potential connection between that box, or something in it, and Victoria's terrifying behaviour. Whatever that connection was, if any, it was beyond my mind to understand it. I steeled myself and pulled down the stairway to gain access to the attic. The wooden steps dropped with a thud and I switched on the light. As I climbed into the attic, a roll of duct tape in my hand, I felt a swirling sensation in my stomach, nerves perhaps. *Get a grip!* I told myself, walking cautiously across the boards to the seemingly normal cardboard box. I wanted to look inside but managed to resist, rolling the tape across the top of the box and sealing it shut. I placed more tape around the edges before turning the box over and added tape to the bottom, on top of the old Sellotape which must have been there for decades.

The box was not heavy, but whatever was inside clanged about as I rotated it and placed it by the attic hatch. I checked my watch; 7.55am. The tip opens at 8am, I recalled. I carried the box down to the hallway and then on into the living room, placing it on the rug in front of where Jessica was sitting. She glanced at it nervously but remained silent.

"I had to park a couple of roads over yesterday," I explained. "I'll bring the car round and get this thing out of here." I was ignored again, and I knew that we needed to have a conversation, but the priority was getting to the tip and fixing up Victoria's bedroom. I'd talk to my wife later.

I brought the car around and double-parked outside the house, leaving the hazard lights on. I dashed inside to grab the package and found it sitting alone on the rug. "Jess?" I called out. Still I got the silent treatment. I muttered a 'fuck's sake' under my breath and made a quick sweep of the house. She had left, with no explanation. Knowing that I couldn't leave the car where it was, I continued with my intentions and picked up the box, sliding it on to the back seat of my car. I then ran back into the house to retrieve a black bag, knowing that if I didn't then the people working at the tip would want the box opened and sorted for recyclables. I squeezed the box into the bag, wrapped duct tape around the neck of the bag to seal it, and drove away.

It was as I arrived at the tip that my phone began to ring. Jessica's name rolled across the screen on the stereo and I hit the answer button for the car's speakers.

"Hey, where did you go?" I asked.

"I'm at the school. They called while you were getting your car." My heart sank, knowing immediately that something was wrong with Victoria. I parked in one of the

299

loading bays and asked what had happened. "The police are here too," Jessica went on, clearly trying to stop herself from crying.

"Shit," was all I could manage.

"Apparently, her tutor was taking the register this morning when Vicky started screaming and smashing her head against the desk. He said she kept shouting to leave her box alone. He tried to restrain her, to stop her hurting herself, but she went for him and scratched his face."

"What time was this?" I asked, seizing the chance to get a word in and already knowing the answer.

"About 7.50," Jessica replied. "It's all happened so fast. She then ran from the classroom, and was found in one of the science labs, turning on the little gas taps they use for Bunsen burners." There was a pause before Jessica said in a whisper, "She told the teachers that, and I quote, 'the flames of Hell are coming'. So now I'm here with teachers, police, and a paramedic, and no one knows what to do with her."

"Look," I started, unsure what advice I could possibly give. "I'm at the tip. I'm getting rid of this damned box and then I'll come to the school. Try not to worry; we'll figure this out. I love you."

300

"Okay," Jessica replied. "See you soon."

I grabbed the bag from the back seat and hurled it into the huge container for general waste. I watched for a few moments as other people added their own rubbish to the heap and, once my bag was safely out of sight, I headed to the school. Victoria had been sat in silence since the incident, refusing to speak to anyone at all, even Jessica. The school itself, and Victoria's tutor, had insisted that they would not press charges, but that she should be looked at by the medical professionals and to take some time off school. Jessica was relaying the events of the previous night to one of the paramedics when I arrived, a very young-looking man who appeared genuinely concerned for my daughter. I shook his hand and asked what he would advise we do.

"I'm not a doctor," he pointed out, "but I would suggest that Victoria sees one. Your wife said that prior to last night's odd behaviour everything had been fine?" He looked at me to confirm, which I did with a nod. "If there was mental illness at play then I would have expected some build-up to these incidents, perhaps smaller behaviours which may have seemed strange but fairly trivial."

"There hasn't been anything that I've noticed," I told him. I looked to Jessica and she shook her head in agreement.

"Then I'd say that seeing a doctor as soon as you can would be wise. Sometimes extreme behaviour like this can be caused by changes in the brain."

"Changes?" Jessica asked. "What sort of changes? How? Oh God," she said, turning to look at me. "Does our baby have a tumour?"

"I'm not saying that," the paramedic said quickly. "I don't want to worry you unnecessarily, but please do get her checked out." He shook my hand, gave Jessica a nod, and walked away leaving us with more questions than answers. We left the school with Victoria, promising to contact the head teacher when we had any news. I had planned for us to make our way straight to the hospital, but Victoria finally spoke, insisting she was too tired and just wanted to sleep. She agreed to let us take her to a doctor the following day.

Once we were home Jessica took Victoria for a bath and put her to bed, hopeful that a good sleep would help things. I took the opportunity to go to the hardware store for the paint and filler, planning to fix the damaged walls that night if Emily would let her sister stay in her room with her. I was relieved to find that the house was almost silent when I returned, the sound of the television on low being all I could make out. I dumped my purchases in the hallway outside of Victoria's room, so as not to disturb her, and paused. The stairs up to the attic were down, but I honestly could not recall whether I had closed the hatch or not that morning.

"Jess," I said quietly as I approached from behind the sofa. "Have you been in the attic?" She looked at me as though I were insane.

"Of course not."

"I thought I had closed it up this morning. Maybe I didn't then. Is Vicky sleeping?"

"I put her to bed after a bath, and I haven't heard anything from her since." It was clear that my wife had been crying, but I could offer no suggestions that would make her feel any better.

"I'll check on her. I got the paint, so once she is up I'll make a start on her room." I crept back along to Victoria's room, opening her bedroom door as quietly as I could, and froze on the spot. Her bed was empty and as soon as I realised that, I heard a creak come from above me. *She's in the fucking attic!* I thought, making my way up there as quickly as I could. The attic was in complete darkness and, for a split-second, I wondered if she was really up there. "Vicky!" I called out, switching on the light.

The room was immediately drenched in light and I almost fell back down the hatch when I saw her. Sitting on the wooden boarded floor was my Victoria, legs crossed, hugging a black bag with duct tape around its opening.

"What are you doing, sweetie?" I asked, keeping my voice low.

"I told you it's my box," she said, her eyes fixed straight ahead.

"Where did you get it?" I asked, knowing that there was no way it could be the same box.

"*He* brought it back to me, after *you* tried to take it away!" Now she looked at me, and I've never seen such a hate-filled look from anyone in my life.

"Who brought it back?" I asked, panic starting to rise within me.

"His name is Hephaestus. He chose me, Daddy. You can't stop him." I backed away, leaving Victoria to cradle her box. I had never heard of Hephaestus, and I could not deny that I was terrified. I went to relay the conversation to Jessica but decided against it. She had been distant, wrought with worry, so I took myself to the kitchen to do some research.

'Hephaestus is the Greek god of Fire. Born deformed, he was cast from heaven. Married to Aphrodite, who had numerous affairs.' *No wonder he's angry,* I thought. I began to wonder what the girls had been learning about at school, whether some history about Greek gods had coincided with a brain tumour and resulted in these incidents. My thoughts were interrupted by Emily returning from school, looking upset.

"Hey," I said. "How was school?"

"Seriously Dad?" she said, rolling her eyes. "Everyone has been going on about Vicky the lunatic; it's embarrassing. But how is she? Do you know what's wrong with her?"

"She's okay," I lied. "We are taking her to a doctor tomorrow. Look, it's probably best if you just leave her to do her own thing for now. She's back in the attic, going through the boxes again."

"Okay," Emily said with a shrug.

"Although," I continued, "would you mind if she stays in your room tonight? I wanted to get hers repainted after the mess she made and haven't had chance yet."

305

"That's fine," Emily said, "as long as she sleeps on the floor and doesn't do any of that weird stuff to my room."

"Agreed," I told her, forcing a smile.

We left Victoria sat in the attic for the following few hours, before coaxing her down for dinner just before 6pm. She hardly ate, moving the food around her plate with her cutlery. Emily had taken us through her day, omitting any gossip about her sister, so we took the opportunity to ask Victoria a few questions.

"Vicky?" I began, trying to tread as softly as I could. I paused while she slowly lifted her head. "Why did you say what you did? About the flames of Hell?" I watched as my daughter stared at me for a moment, as if trying to process my question, before her face lit up in a grin that could only be described as sinister.

"The flames of Hell are coming," she stated, unblinking, still making eye contact with me. Before I could respond, she repeated the phrase, again and again, louder and louder. "The flames of Hell are coming, the flames of Hell are coming, the flames of Hell are coming." Then came the laughter; maniacal, frightening laughter which sent Emily running to her bedroom in tears. Jessica had no words to offer, just a look of sadness on her face. I could do nothing except change the subject.

"I'm going to paint your bedroom tonight," I explained. "So, it may be best if you sleep in the living room, if you don't mind?" I had changed my mind about letting the girls share, and I was certain that Emily would not be keen after the outburst.

"I don't mind. It won't matter anyway."

"What do you mean?" I asked, getting no reply. "Look, Vicky, we'll see a doctor tomorrow and get to the bottom of this, okay?" For a split-second it appeared that my little girl was back as she told me 'okay', with a sullen nod. *We just need to get through the night,* I told myself, wondering if it would be best for Jessica to stay in the living room with Victoria. As hard as it was to admit, I didn't want anyone around her at that point because I was scared of her.

We settled the girls down at the usual time, Jessica and myself retiring to bed early to let Vicky sleep. I had lost all motivation for redecorating and decided to put it off for another day. As with the previous night, it took a long time to get to sleep, but this night the sleep was interrupted by billowing smoke. The toxicity of the smoke had hit us hard while

307

we slept, the bedroom door would not budge, and we were too weak to escape. I had no doubt that Victoria, or whatever had taken her over, had unleashed *the flames of Hell* on our home. I positioned myself beside my wife who was barely conscious, shed a tear for Emily and prayed that she had met a swift end if she hadn't made a miraculous escape. I wondered about Victoria, sure that she must have started the fire and left the scene. Part of me hoped that she would die with us on that night, not as punishment but to spare her from a lifetime in an institute as that would surely be her fate. Perhaps she did die, perhaps she disappeared into the night intent on bringing the flames of Hell to others. I will never know.

# Burt's Rage

A scream rang out, audible even over the sounds of the milling crowd. The shopping centre was packed as always, a persistent hum of chatter filling the air. The scream was followed quickly by a second, and a third, before panic set in. It seemed as though hundreds of people all shrieked in unison before stampeding for the exit. The only person not showing signs of panic was the old man as he sat on a bench in the middle of the concourse, coffee in hand. If anyone had been paying him any attention, they may have noticed a small smile attempting to move at the corners of his mouth. As he watched the woman flail about in circles, attempting to douse the flames that covered her from head to toe, his expression remained virtually unchanged. The stench of burning flesh had filled the shopping centre as the woman dropped to her knees, before falling limply to the ground. The smoke set off the overhead sprinklers, a little too late, and this led to another shriek from the crowds as they were showered with cold water. Satisfied the woman was dead, the old man slowly made his way out, coffee still in hand.

If anyone knew of the man's power, they could easily mistake him for a demon or some other hellish abomination. But Burt was just a man like any other, aside from the fact that his anger could be manifested in more... *unusual* ways. If asked, he would be unable to explain when it had started. Perhaps it had always been there but had needed that one event to reveal itself, that single moment of pure, uncontrollable rage – his wife's infidelity. He'd never seen it coming, foolishly believing her to be content with him. There had been no time for apologies from her, for shouting from him. There was simply a moment of painful silence as all three parties considered their situation, followed by an eruption of flames.

The bed, Burt's wife, her lover (unknown to Burt), ignited in an instant. As much as one may try to scream when ablaze, it's not easy at all. Flames lick at the gums and tongue, vaporising saliva and destroying vocal cords in an instant. Due to the close proximity of Burt's wife and the other man, their burning flesh melded into one another before they could even try to stand. Burt watched on, his initial shock turning to bemusement as the couple stopped moving and flames began to creep up the curtains beside the bed. With a sigh, Burt grabbed his phone and called the fire brigade.

He had no intention of running, despite knowing he'd be the prime suspect should anyone suggest foul play. Nobody did. Burt was respected and liked in the small town and everyone rallied round to offer condolences and sympathy. Poor Burt, not only losing his home to a fire but also his wife. And not only losing her, finding out she was unfaithful too. How devastated he must be!

*** 

Try as he might over the next few years, Burt could never muster enough anger to start a fire. In fact, it was almost eight years before he felt anger like that again. He'd been walking home late, something that had never bothered him before, when he heard shouting from above him. He'd cut through a short alley which ran alongside a multistorey car park and although he knew it was a hangout for teenagers, he'd never had any problems with them. Another shout came, this time more aggressive, and Burt looked up out of instinct. Leaning over the second floor were three youngsters, possibly two boys and girl but it was hard to make out in the dark and through their hoodies.

"Oi, Mister! Got a couple of quid?" came the shout. There was nothing friendly in the request and Burt decided it best to just not reply. He'd taken three or four steps when he felt a thud on the back of his head, followed by the crash of a bottle hitting the pavement beside him. The force was enough for him to stagger a few steps forward but he managed to keep on his feet. He paused, weighing up the options, trying to calm his racing pulse, but it was useless. Burt took a step forward, laughter burst out from above him, and he lost it.

Turning to face the offenders, Burt couldn't help but smile. The bigger lad, the one who had shouted, started to say something else. The aggression coming off these kids was palpable. Society would be better off without them, of this Burt had no doubt. Before they could even step away from the concrete wall, the dark was illuminated by three bright flashes. Burt noticed this time that the fire didn't appear to start in any one particular area – it was as though the whole body combusted at once. Burt held his position, watching for those few seconds as the teenagers flailed about, bumping into one another, and then dropping out of sight as they fell behind the wall. Burt made his way home, a full grin on his face.

Old age can bring about a generally less jovial mood. Things that would have merely been an annoyance five years ago now made Burt angry and anger would lead to death – that much was inevitable. Burt had considered trying to control it but he had no real interest in that; he felt no remorse for the deaths, feebly justifying it by telling himself it was out of his hands. He was certainly aware how strange it must appear, for all these bizarre deaths, but nobody sane was about to suggest Burt was behind it all.

The following years were carnage – drivers neglecting to indicate ended up in burnt out cars, rude couriers would rarely make their next delivery, even people on the television (politicians, especially) would mysteriously die in fires. The only incident Burt felt a twinge of regret about was the bus driver. He'd been a horrible person, that was undeniable, but Burt's fiery rage led to the bus crashing and a lot of people getting hurt.

***

All this brings us back to today, with Burt now walking away from a shopping

313

centre as emergency services vehicles scream past. The burnt woman would be identified, would probably appear on the evening news. *Had she been that awful?* Burt wondered. *After all, she only knocked into me as she rushed past.* He shrugged. *She only needed to say sorry. Manners cost nothing, but a lack of them can be deadly.*

# Home

In June of 1987 I was six years old. My parents had decided to uproot my sister and I from the city and relocate to a more rural setting. At six, I didn't particularly care. I had only a few friends and was much happier spending my days playing outdoors and exploring, than being restricted to our tiny garden at the old house. My sister had little to say on the subject of moving as she was three at the time and cared little for anything besides her dolls. The house felt huge to me at that time, and even now I guess that it's larger than the average home. Dating back almost two hundred years, the house was in need of redecoration, but it was a superb place to explore, filled with nooks and crannies.

I remember the smell to this day - it reminded me of charity shops and attics. It was an 'old' smell, if such a thing exists; musty, unloved even. My parents had a removals company deal with the job of relocating us, and I don't recall being asked to help in any way with carrying boxes or small items that my six-year-old frame could have managed. Perhaps it was easier with me out of the way, so I spent the first few days exploring the house and the grounds.

I know now that the land which came with the house spanned several acres, but in 1987 I just saw it as an almost endless patch of English countryside which was now mine. There were a few large trees, oak I believe, and I practically begged Father to build me a treehouse in one of them. I actually suggested we build two treehouses, opposite one another, and that he should construct a zip-line between them. That never happened, much to my disappointment. At the far end of the property I discovered a tyre-swing which had been hung from one of the oaks, the remains of a broken greenhouse, and a well which appeared to have been long neglected.

Having moved in June, I was pulled from my schooling before the official end of term. Of course, a new school place had been arranged but, as this was not available until September, I was lucky enough to enjoy a doubly long summer break. I knew no one, but happily occupied myself climbing about in the tall trees and swinging lazily on the tyre. I made maps of the grounds, smearing them with damp teabags to create an aged appearance, claiming they were treasure maps.

I talked Mother into buying me a rather fancy notebook one day when we had visited the nearest shop, and I spent many weeks filling it with sketches of flowers and insects that I found during my explorations. My parents had been clear on the rules, of which there were only two: keep within the boundaries of our property, as they did not know who owned the neighbouring land and did not want me getting into trouble, and keep away from the well. I had understood the need to stay on our own property but did ask why I was not to go near the well.

"Why do you think?" Father had replied. "If you fall down it then you may never get back out. God only knows what's down there. Filthy water, rats, monsters, even." He said this last word with a wink, thankfully, but I could understand the concern. Unfortunately, the mystery of what was down the well only served to make it all the more tempting and I decided that soon I would see how close I could get to it without ending up in trouble. Fearful of my parents telling me I was no longer allowed to explore with such freedom, I obeyed them for as long as I could. I knew, however, that I could not keep away from the well forever.

The maps that I had created all included the well, but I had never gotten closer than perhaps twenty feet from its old flint walls. Until the day I did. Mother and Father had guests, someone that Father worked with and that man's wife, I think. I knew they would be focused on entertaining, and it was expected that I would be outside, climbing a tree or drawing a butterfly. While the adults chatted over clinking glasses in the sitting room, I crept around the house filling my satchel with items I believed would be of use. I took the torch from my bedroom, found a ball of twine in Mother's craft supplies, as well as a length of measuring tape. I felt nervous as I left through the back door, that fluttering of the stomach that you get when engaging in an activity you should not be doing, but I wandered across towards the tyre swing as casually as possible.

I waited on the swing for what felt like an age to my six-year-old mind, but was, in reality, around twenty minutes. I spent the time sketching the well from where I sat, capturing the grey of the flint rocks in the wall, and the pure blackness of the opening. From where I sat it looked too black. Stuffing my notebook back into my satchel, I began taking steps towards the well. Every few feet I looked up at the house, afraid that I had been spotted, but no one paid me any attention. I reached the flint wall and placed a hand on it, adrenalin pumping through me at this simple act of defiance against my parents.

Looking down into the darkness made me feel queasy. I had no real fear of heights, after all I was happy climbing up into the oak trees, but perhaps it was because I could not see through the darkness. It was impossible to tell how far down it went, or what lie within the complete blackness. Of course, this was what I had expected, and was the reason I had brought a torch. I smiled, congratulating myself on my ingenuity, and clicked the torch on. The beam pierced through the darkness to a reasonable distance, illuminating the flint walls which appeared to continue downward even further than the light would show. Whatever lie at the bottom of the well, whether that be stagnant water or simply dried up earth, was too far for my torch to reach.

On to part two of my plan - the ball of twine. I had no idea how long the twine was, but it was a fairly large ball. I had used a similar one to join two of the big trees together (in order to keep out invaders when I was playing pirates), and they were a good distance apart. I had no doubt that the twine would reach the bottom of the well and, when it did, I would be able to measure the distance. I tied a small rock to one end of the twine and slowly lowered it into the darkness, careful not to let it drop.

My arms began to ache as the twine moved slowly between my hands and I came close to just pulling the thing back up, but eventually the twine felt different, heavier even. Now, I may have only been six, but I was not stupid. My mind had been racing as I lowered that rock into the pit, and I knew that the twine would go slack if the base of the well was dry. The change in the pull and the increased weight made me certain that the rock had reached water, which was no real surprise; it was a well, after all. Excitedly, I began to extract the rock. Fighting gravity on the way up was much harder than I had expected, but eventually I could see it and pulled it over the wall of the well and on to the grass beneath my feet.

I found the rock to be wet, as I'd expected. I sniffed it, and it reminded me of dirty ditches, of water which had been left unmoved for too long. I stretched out

Mother's measuring tape to its fullest and placed the rock at one end. From there, I was able to measure the twine from the rock to the part which I had been holding when I felt it hit the water, in two-metre increments. I pulled out my notebook, writing *Well - 21 metres*. That's a long way to fall, I recall thinking, as I picked up the twine (rock still attached) and headed back to the tyre-swing to think about what I had learned. That was the night it had started.

*** 

I used to dream a lot as a child, but they were always happy dreams; pirates, jungle adventures, dinosaurs, and trips to space were usually the theme. Some dreams even incorporated all of these. The night after my experiment with the well I had the first nightmare that I can remember. In the dream I was back at the well, repeating the task with the rock and the twine, only this time it was different. I lowered the rock, felt the difference in its weight, began pulling it back up. Only the rock was no longer there. In its place was a doll, plastic eyes missing, dress dripping with stagnant water, the twine wrapped around its neck as though it had been a victim of the gallows.

I awoke screaming that night, much to the concern of my mother who brought me into her bed and comforted me. She asked what the dream had been about, but I would not tell her, afraid that she would know I had disobeyed her and strayed too close to the well. That dream stuck with me all the following day, and I kept away from the well, opting to play indoors with my sister.

We spent some time drawing and colouring, her efforts comprising of swirls of colour on large sheets of paper. I drew in my notebook and it was not until Father asked what I was doing that I saw it myself. It appeared that I had spent the entire afternoon drawing the exact image of the doll from my nightmare, over and over, on page after page. As the image came into focus, I burst into tears, running to my room and throwing myself on to my bed. For the first time in my short life, I felt truly afraid, but still I kept the truth from my parents.

I told my mother that I was worried about having another bad dream, but she would not allow me to stay in her bed again. I think this came more from Father, as I heard him saying something about me having to grow up a bit. I lay awake for a long time, the face of that disfigured doll at the forefront of my mind, when I heard tiny footsteps outside my room. I sat up in bed, frozen, staring at the door as it slowly began to open. I knew the footsteps were too light to belong to an adult and the only thought my terrified brain could come up with was that the doll had come to find me. I must have been holding my breath because I let out a huge sigh of relief as I saw my sister standing in the doorway.

She made her way to the side of my bed, hands behind her back, not speaking. It wasn't until she reached me that I could see her eyes were closed and I wondered if she were sleepwalking. Then it happened, something which should not have been possible. My sister pulled her hands round in front of her, revealing what she had been hiding behind her back. She threw the abomination of a doll onto my bed, its clothing still dripping, eyeless face staring up at me. I'll remember my sister's words for all my life - *Elizabeth wants to go home.* With that, she scurried out of my room, giggling in a way I'd never heard her do before. I did the only sensible thing then...I screamed.

Mother and Father both came to me this time and I told them everything. There was no sense in hiding it and I no longer cared if I was not allowed out to play. There was no way I wanted to go anywhere near that awful well again. I explained that I had gone to the well, that I had measured how deep it went, and the nightmare I had the previous night. They saw the doll, spreading a patch of water across my duvet. I was relieved that they could actually see the thing, and that it was not just in my head. Perhaps it would have been better if the doll had not been real, but I did not think so at the time. I told them what my sister had said, and Mother went to check on her. She was asleep and no one had heard her get out of bed.

My parents settled me down as well as they could, Father taking the doll. He said he would get rid of it, but I could see the concern on his face. I told him to throw it in the well. He said that he would, but I didn't know if he was telling the truth until the morning. I did not sleep well that night, waking several times and feeling afraid, but I could not recall the contents of my nightmares. However, morning brought another scream from my lips as I opened my eyes and found myself face to face with the doll on my pillow.

Father insisted he had put the doll into the bin, outside the house. I told him again, begged in fact, that he take it to the well. I cried and cried, doing the best I could to convince him, and finally he relented. He may well have thought throwing a doll into a well was pointless, but I suppose he could see no harm in doing it either. I watched him walk out of the back door, as I climbed on to the kitchen worktop to watch from the perceived safety of the house. I saw him approach the well, give a quick glance back towards the house, and drop the doll in. I must have looked away for only a moment, but when I looked back, I could not see Father. I ran to the door to see if he was on his way, but he was nowhere in sight. My mother and sister never saw him again.

***

Mother was frantic, running around the house and across the land outside calling Father's name. She shouted down into the well but there was no response and she was left with little choice but to involve the police. They came, of course, but were convinced that Father had simply had enough and walked away, that he would probably be in a pub and would turn up eventually. Mother knew this would not be the case and managed to convince the

325

policemen to check the well. The only explanation could be that he had somehow fallen in. I watched from my position in the kitchen as the policemen shone their torches into the well and called out, all to no avail. They left us there, completely unable to understand what had happened, lost without Father's presence. Daylight turned to dusk with no developments, until my sister spoke up during our tea.

"Elizabeth wants to go home," she told us. I looked to Mother, the fear evident on my face. Mother paused, seemingly thinking about what to say to a three-year-old.

"Who's Elizabeth, honey?" she asked, her sing-song tone almost hiding her concern.

"Elizabeth dolly," my sister replied, smiling.

"That dolly was called Elizabeth?" Mother asked. My sister shook her head. "It was Elizabeth's dolly?" Mother tried again. My sister nodded, before repeating *Elizabeth wants to go home*. "And where is Elizabeth now?" We watched as my sister climbed down from her seat at the dining table and made her way to the kitchen. She placed a foot on the handle of one of the lower cupboards and hoisted herself

326

on to the worktop before pointing out of the window - pointing at the well.

"Elizabeth is in the well?" Mother asked, not believing there to be any truth to this but wanting to understand what my sister was implying. "How do you know this?"

"Elizabeth dolly told me," my sister stated with a smile full of sadness. Mother told us both to finish our food while she went to make a telephone call. I could make out parts of the conversation, discussions of the well, of someone coming to look into it properly. I recall her saying that she knew it sounded insane, but that she wanted to be sure there was nothing, and nobody, down there.

***

The following morning, I awoke to the eyeless plastic face of Elizabeth's doll once again soaking my pillow. There was still no sign of Father, and Mother burst into tears at the sight of the doll. I wanted to ask her to throw it back into the well but was too afraid in case she disappeared like Father. Nonetheless, I knew the doll had to go back, and for my Mother's safety I decided that I should be the one to take it. I ran from the house before Mother could tell me to stop, stomping the dew-soaked grass beneath my bare feet, jaw set in determination. As I reached the well, I peered inside to find it even more black and terrifying than it had been that first time.

"Father!" I screamed into the void. No reply. "Elizabeth! I have your stupid doll!" There was anger in my voice as I hurled the doll into the well and waited for the sound of it hitting the water below. When I turned away, I had expected to see Mother following me, ready to send me back indoors, but she was not there. The early morning daylight had faded to darkness in an instant, a cold wind had risen, seemingly out of nowhere, and the house looked ... different, newer perhaps.

I knew that something was very wrong and ran back to the house, shivering in the night air, and bolted inside. I called out for Mother but heard no response. I darted from room to room, all of which were unfamiliar, decorated in a different manner, furnishings I did not recognise. It was my house, yet it was not. The entire ground floor was empty of people, so I searched the bedrooms. In what should have been my room, were only boxes of junk. My sister's room was strange - still a room for a young girl, but not how it had been only moments earlier. The last room to check was the master bedroom, in which I found a man and a woman whom I had never seen before. They looked at me with both shock and confusion as I swung the door open. They were sitting on the edge of the bed, the woman crying into her husband's shoulder.

"Who are you?" he demanded from me, just as I was about to ask the same question.

"I live here," I said meekly, unsure if this was still the truth. "Where's Mother?"

"You have the wrong house," the man told me, before grabbing my arm and dragging me down the stairs. "Came to steal from us, did you?" I tried to protest, attempting to explain but it is difficult to do so when you don't understand what is happening yourself. Then I asked a question. I don't know where it came from really, but it felt like the right thing to say.

"Where's Elizabeth?"

The man froze as we reached the bottom of the stairs, a glint of anger and panic in his eyes.

"How do you know Elizabeth?" he asked.

"Where is she?" I repeated. The man glanced to the upper floor as if he did not want to be seen. He dragged me out of the front door and across the grass. I tried to free myself from his grip, but I was too weak at that age.

"You want to see Elizabeth? Fine." I was pulled to the edge of the well. The man placed his hands under my arms and lifted me over the wall, holding me for a moment above that pure blackness. I felt my pyjama bottoms becomes damp as my bladder released and all I could think was how far down the pit went. Then he let go.

*** 

There was a rush of wind past my ears as I fell, my stomach making that odd sensation one gets on fairground rides, and my arms battering against the coarse flint walls. It took only a matter of seconds before I hit the water below, plummeting beneath the surface. I managed to get my head above water and take in air, but I was in agony and knew I wouldn't be able to bob on the surface for long. The darkness was impenetrable, the smell almost unbearable, but I could feel other 'things' in the water, just below the water line.

I tried to use the larger item to keep me afloat, but it appeared to sink further whenever I touched it. It was soft in places and, at first, I thought it was a large bag. I felt my way around its shape until I touch something that brought vomit to my mouth. The shape I could feel in that icy water was undeniably a nose; a nose which was clearly still part of a head. I ran my hand across what felt like lips, down to a neck which felt as though it had been ripped open. A little further below this wound I found the unmistakable shape of a tie. Father's tie.

I began to weep, which is almost impossible when trying to keep afloat. I hugged the corpse of my father and screamed for my mother, who never came to my aid. I knew that the other thing floating in the water was Elizabeth, but I had no intention of letting go of my Father just to feel the rotten remains of a stranger. Her father may have been a monster, but mine was my hero. My strength gave out as Father's body began to sink further into the earth and I went with it.

And now *I* want to go home.

# Dark Waters

We'd ended up in Romania almost by accident. There was finally an end in sight to the damn pandemic and global travel options were starting to open up. After more than two years without a break away, Martha and I took a fortnight off work and caught a train to the airport with just a backpack each. Financially, the pandemic had been a blessing with little to spend any money on, so we knew we could pretty much go wherever we wanted. The idea was to head to Gatwick and get on whichever flight was leaving next. This happened to be Bucharest.

We boarded that flight with a mixture of excitement and nervousness. We had no accommodation booked, no knowledge of the country at all, and no idea what to expect. Martha could sense my trepidation but put my mind at ease – she was good like that.

"We can just mooch about for a day or two and if we don't like it we'll fly somewhere else."

I nodded, knowing she was right but not wanting to spend the whole fortnight on planes looking for the best places. "We'll see," I replied. "I'm sure there will be plenty to do." I wasn't wrong. Bucharest was impressive, with outstanding architecture and plenty of boutique shops and eateries. It wasn't until the third day that we started looking at trips further afield.

We skipped the guided walks around the city, certain we'd seen everything by that point, but we did book ticket for the *Ghosts & Vampires Tour* on that evening. It was as expected but still enjoyable as we joined another ten tourists for a walk around supposedly haunted locations in the centre of the city, guided by an enthusiastic Romanian man wearing a vampire-style cape. When the tour was over, he handed me a leaflet with details of the 12-hour trip to see Dracula's Castle.

"We can't come all the way here and not visit the castle," Martha said, and I knew she was right. She'd said the same thing in Venice about the gondola trip.

"We'll go back in the morning and book it," I told her. "It's getting late and I'm hungry." We stopped at a small pub which was only a few doors along from the hotel we were staying at, having been there for lunch when we'd first arrived. I didn't know what anything on the menu was, but the beer was cheap and we'd had some local soup last time. That's where we meant Florin.

He was slouched at the bar, almost looking like a part of the furniture. I didn't pay him any attention until he spoke, sensing my difficulty in selecting a local drink to sample. He pointed out a strange looking bottle covered in dust. "Try that, my friend. Good, local," Florin said in broken English. I didn't like the look of the drink but ordered two anyway in an attempt to be polite. "English?" he asked, and I nodded. "Seeing the sights?" I could see I wouldn't get away without speaking.

"We've been around the city and we'll probably take a trip to Dracula's Castle. Is there anywhere else you'd recommend?"

"Bigar Falls," he said after a moment's thought. "It's waterfall. Very pretty, very romantic." He grinned at this last part, his eyes flicking towards Martha.

"Sounds nice," I replied. "Do they run tours from the city?"

"Yes, but much money. They take advantage, take too much money."

"Well, that's to be expected. These trips always cost a lot."

"I take you tomorrow, much cheaper in my car. Tourist trips only go in daytime. Waterfall better at night."

I didn't know how to respond so I told

him I'd talk to Martha and see what she thought. I expected her to say no, that she'd feel safer through a proper tour operator, but she didn't. "Sounds good to me, more authentic. He probably just wants to make some money and it'll cost us less. And if it's nicer there after dark..."

All I could think about were horror films where Western tourists get kidnapped and harvested for organs, but I pushed it out my mind as best I could. *Just movies,* I told myself. As it turned out, Martha was right. Florin was just looking to make a bit of money for beer by driving us out to the falls.

The journey was several hours and we didn't leave until early evening. I'm sure Florin had been drinking before we left but decided not to say anything, worried about making the journey awkward. It wasn't long before we were out of the city and onto darkened country lanes, unable to see anything but the gravel roads illuminated by the car's headlights. I wondered how much of the waterfall we'd be able to see in the darkness but had assumed it would be lit up if it was a tourist attraction.

I was right about the lighting but I'd expected to see other people. Florin stopped the car and the waterfall was visible from where we were, maybe two hundred metres away. We all needed a toilet break but the public ones designed for the tour groups were now locked so we had to find a spot in the darkness to relieve ourselves, Martha included.

"How close can you get?" Martha asked, gazing upon the impressive falls. It was huge, falling around an enormous, moss-covered rock the size of a large house. Pastel coloured spotlights had been installed just above the surface level of the river below, sending sparkling shards of light through the misty water.

"There is pathway, like bridge. It goes through waterfall. Right inside," Florin told us. We followed as he clicked on a torch and began walking along the darkened path.

"Are we allowed to be here?" I asked, not so much worried about Florin but concerned we were trespassing and would end up in a Romanian jail.

"Of course! Public place, yes? Natural, not owned." He had a point but the gate at the end of the boardwalk suggested otherwise, a large padlock holding it firmly locked. Florin didn't seem fazed, pulling a metal contraption from his pocket and fiddling with the padlock. I heard it click open and looked at Martha, unable to hide my trepidation.

She shrugged and whispered in my ear. "Live a little," she ordered, before pulling me by the hand and following Florin along the bridge. At the entrance to the waterfall, we all darted through the sheet of water, trying not to get soaked through before the long trip back. Inside, it was incredible. It was probably the most wonderful place we had ever been to – the water falling around us was, unexpectedly, almost silent, the air smelled sweet, and it felt comfortably warmer that outside of that special place.

Florin stood grinning. "I give you some time, maybe half hour? Then we return. Is that enough?" I thought about it and, as beautiful as the place was, there wasn't all that much to do.

"Ok," I nodded.

"You two have good time, yeah?" Florin said as he darted back through to the bridge and I knew exactly what he thought Martha and I would be doing. Truth be told, I hadn't even considered it but making love under this waterfall did sound like an excellent idea. I took Martha's hand, moving in to kiss her, but she was hesitant. "He's probably watching," she said. "You know if it was safe then I'd be more than happy to. But the thought of him sitting in his car with binoculars in one hand and his dick in the other is quite off-putting."

I sighed. "I very much doubt that's what he's doing, but I know what you mean." I sat myself down on the damp rock, water falling to both sides as well as ahead, and Martha joined me. "It really is lovely."

"Yes," she smiled, nestling her head on my shoulder. We sat for a while, snuggled and content, before Martha glanced at her watch. "Shit, it's been forty minutes."

I pulled myself up with a groan, stretching my back and cursing my lack of exercise during the pandemic. Hand-in-hand, we rushed through the chilly water and back on to the bridge. Martha was in front of me so reached the gate first. She pushed but it didn't move. She shoved harder. Nothing. Gently, I pulled her back to allow me access. Thumping the gate, all I could hear was the rattle of the padlock. Fencing had been added to both sides of the gate which I'm certain wasn't there when we entered. Although it didn't look impossible, it would not be easy to climb it and the river below now seemed malevolent, angry, and hungry.

"Florin!" Martha shouted. Silence. "What do we do?" she asked, turning to me.

I placed my arms around her. "Fucking scammer," I muttered. We'd paid Florin for the round trip and he'd clearly thought it hilarious to shut us in and abandon us. "Not a lot we can do. Either we try to force the gate, climb around it, or we wait until someone comes."

Martha looked down into the darkness of the river. "Climbing is dangerous. We'll just have to stick it out until morning and explain what happened. I don't think we'll be in trouble, they'll just put it down to stupid tourists and send us back to the hotel."

I gave the gate a few hard kicks but nothing gave. The hour was late and we were many miles from Bucharest. Even if we could get through the gate, I was unsure we'd be any better off. The thought of roaming the countryside of a unknow place made me nervous, especially knowing we were too far from the hotel to simply walk back. At least there would be people arriving here in the morning, all we could do would be to make the most of it, enjoy the beauty of the waterfall and try to ignore the swirling river below us.

Huddled in that damp space, clothing wet, a chill creeping into my bones, it took all my effort to remain upbeat. This *could* be quite romantic, and certainly a memorable event, but I was convinced the sounds of the river were growing louder. It had been barely noticeable when we'd arrived, like strolling past a stream. Now, Martha struggled to make herself heard, even with her mouth so close to my face.

Eventually, despite the discomfort and noise, we fell into a fitful sleep on the cold stone floor. I couldn't say how long I had slept but two things were immediately obvious when I did awaken – the river was quiet, babbling gently below, and Martha was gone. It took a fraction of a second to realise this – the area in which we had slept was too small for me to simply not notice her, and the bridge was empty. I leapt to my feet, heart hammering, and raced along to the gate. My hope, of course, was that she had found a way to open it, but I was unable to fathom why she would have left me there. The gate was as it had been when we fell asleep – cold, defiant, immovable.

A wave of nausea hit me as I glanced down into the murky water below. Down was the only other way to go, the only way Martha could have gone. But why? How? And, most importantly, where was she now? I weighed up my options, not liking any of them. I certainly was not keen on the idea of jumping down to the river, unsure if I'd even survive the leap. I reasoned that my best bet would be to try to climb the security fence – if I fell then I'd end up in the river anyway, but if I made it then I'd find another way down there, for Martha surely had to be nearby. The current wasn't strong anymore, perhaps she had injured herself falling and needed my help.

I negotiated the fence with less difficulty than I'd expected, always underestimating my own physical strength and now cursing myself for not climbing it in the first place. Maybe it would have been futile, maybe Martha would not have managed it safely, and where would we even had gone? I followed the path quickly, finding myself back where Florin had parked the car. I felt that same surge of panic as I saw it, the car still where it had been left. *He hasn't left us here,* I realised. This only led to more nightmarish thoughts running through my head as I understood something must have happened to him.

"Florin!" I yelled. "Martha!" Silence. Cautiously, I approached the car, testing the driver's door. Locked. Cupping my hands against the window, I peered in. Nothing. I spun around trying to find a way down to the river and noticed a small clearing next to an information post. Breaking into a jog, I headed towards the opening in the bushes but something on the sign caught my eye. Under the weak moonlight, the text was difficult to make out, but the images were not. Perhaps it was the glimpse of flesh that caught the attention of my male brain, the naked breasts in the image calling out to me. The sign had no text in English, so it didn't matter about the darkness. What it did contain were two images – on the left was a stereotypical mermaid, a pretty, topless woman with the tail of a fish. The image on the right reminded me of the movie *Gremlins;* the mermaid was there again but the skin looked mottled, grey breasts hung limply to her waist, her face riddled with pus and her mouth filled with dagger-sharp teeth.

I shook my head before hurrying to the riverbank. I stumbled in the dark, tripping on branches and other detritus. I scanned up and down, unable to see anything that would help. I turned to my right and began walking, my eyes moving between the surface of the river and the ground before me. If I could find Florin then great, but Martha was my priority. I decided that directly beneath the waterfall would be a logical place to start looking.

It was as I passed beneath the footbridge that I tripped again, this time landing on the damp grass. I turned, instinctively, to see what I'd fallen over. At first glance it looked like a thick branch, so I began to look away from it. Something caught in the light, a reflection of moonlight hitting the end of the item. Still on my knees, I moved a little closer, catching the reflection again. The golden light bounced from the ring, the chunky, eighteen karat piece of metal that Florin had been wearing on his right index finger. I crawled a few inches further to see that the ring was still on Florin's finger, a finger still attached to Florin's hand which, in turn, was still attached to what I thought was a branch. The arm, however, was no longer a part of Florin, wherever he may be. I vomited.

This new knowledge flooded my brain in a fraction of second; Florin hadn't left us, something was out there, Martha is undeniably in danger, if she's even still alive. I focussed my hunt on Martha but knew I'd have to look for the rest of Florin's body, if only to locate the keys to his car. I pulled myself to my weak legs and took a few unsteady steps forward, scanning the riverbank, the water's surface, the rocks which rose to the area

343

we had slept on. Nothing. I called out, only to be met by silence.

I wandered the edge of the river for what felt like hours, back and forth, seeing nothing. I debated giving up, my grief beginning to pull at me as the inevitable clawed at my mind. As if from nowhere, a song pierced the silence. Hypnotic, alluring, sinister. The tune could not be ignored, as much as my mind screamed *no*. If I left, tried to make a run for it, I'd always wonder if that was her, if I could have saved Martha. I couldn't bring myself to abandon her, despite the fear gnawing at me. I followed the sound as it echoed within the trees and off the rocks, trying desperately to find its origin. Before too long, I found myself at the base of the waterfall once again. The song was louder here, clear within the darkness. What had begun as only a tune now contained words. I couldn't understand them all and I presumed they were in the local language, but something stood out, two words that I was all too familiar with – my name.

"Martha!" I called out again. "Is that you?" A stirring on the surface caught my eye, ripples forming. I was frozen to the spot as something began to rise from the water. Hair, long and flowing despite the wetness, a face, instantly recognisable. That smile, one I'd kissed goodnight every evening for years, greeted me. "Martha?" I said again, this time with confusion. She did not speak and it became clear the tune wasn't coming from her. She swam towards me and I had no doubts it was her. My first thought was a mix of optimism and hope – perhaps she had climbed down to the river while I slept, choosing to go for a moonlit swim. Not that it explained the dismembered arm, but it gave me some hope, even if that was to be short-lived.

A couple of feet from the riverbank she stopped, rising far enough out of the water for me to see her naked breasts. She motioned with her head for me to join her before swimming out further. "You come to me," I said. "Something happened to Florin, we need to find his keys and get out of here." Martha bobbed in the water, still smiling but offering no reply. I didn't know what to do – I couldn't leave her there, but I had no intention of getting in the water. I pleaded, begged, even sobbed. Martha would not come to me, just smiling insanely as the tune continued to float around us.

"Then I'm leaving," I said. "I'll find the keys and get help. I just want you to come out of the water." Martha looked as though she were considering my words, deciding if I was bluffing or not. In truth, I didn't know if I'd actually leave her like that, alone and naked in a strange place. There was an almost imperceptible nod from her before she began swimming towards me once more. I breathed a sigh of relief, stretching my arms out to help her climb the bank. There was no need to offer assistance.

Within seconds she was on me, having thrust her muscular tail and launched herself onto the land. It took a moment for my brain to process what I was seeing as the beautiful face of my lover turned pale and grotesque. The smile remained, but as the lips parted, the razor-sharp teeth from the image I'd seen earlier came into view. As I felt the skin on my neck tear open and I could only wonder if this abomination was actually Martha or if I'd been tricked by an illusion. I'd never find out.

## Also from Red Cape Publishing

## Anthologies:

*Elements of Horror Book One: Earth*
*Elements of Horror Book Two: Air*
*Elements of Horror Book Three: Fire*
*Elements of Horror Book Four: Water*
*A is for Aliens: A to Z of Horror Book One*
*B is for Beasts: A to Z of Horror Book Two*
*C is for Cannibals: A to Z of Horror Book Three*
*D is for Demons: A to Z of Horror Book Four*
*E is for Exorcism: A to Z of Horror Book Five*
*F is for Fear: A to Z of Horror Book Six*
*G is for Genies: A to Z of Horror Book Seven*
*H is for Hell: A to Z of Horror Book Eight*
*It Came From the Darkness: A Charity Anthology*

## Short Story Collections:

*Embrace the Darkness by P.J. Blakey-Novis*
*Tunnels by P.J. Blakey-Novis*
*The Artist by P.J. Blakey-Novis*
*Karma by P.J. Blakey-Novis*
*The Place Between Worlds by P.J. Blakey-Novis*
*Short Horror Stories by P.J. Blakey-Novis*
*Home by P.J. Blakey-Novis*
*Keep It Inside by Mark Anthony Smith*

## Novelettes:

*The Ivory Tower by Antoinette Corvo*

## Novellas:

*Four by P.J. Blakey-Novis*
*Dirges in the Dark by Antoinette Corvo*
*The Cat That Caught The Canary by Antoinette Corvo*
*Bow-Legged Buccaneers from Outer Space by David Owain Hughes*

## Novels:

*Madman Across the Water by Caroline Angel*
*Madman Across the Water: The Curse Awakens by Caroline Angel*
*Less by Caroline Angel*
*Where Shadows Move by Caroline Angel*
*The Broken Doll by P.J. Blakey-Novis*
*The Broken Doll: Shattered Pieces by P.J. Blakey-Novis*
*The Vegas Rift by David F. Gray*

## Children's Books:

*Grace & Bobo: The Trip to the Future by Peter Blakey-Novis*
*The Little Bat That Could by Gemma Paul*
*The Mummy Walks at Midnight by Gemma Paul*
*A Very Zombie Christmas by Gemma Paul*

## Follow Red Cape Publishing

www.redcapepublishing.com
www.facebook.com/redcapepublishing
www.twitter.com/redcapepublish
www.instagram.com/redcapepublishing
www.pinterest.co.uk/redcapepublishing
www.patreon.com/redcapepublishing